PRESSBURGER, G.

GRANTA BOOKS

THE LAW OF WHITE SPACES

ALSO BY GIORGIO PRESSBURGER

Homage to the Eighth District
(with Nicola Pressburger)

GIORGIO PRESSBURGER

THE LAW OF
WHITE SPACES

TRANSLATED FROM THE ITALIAN
BY PIERS SPENCE

GRANTA BOOKS
LONDON
in association with
PENGUIN BOOKS

GRANTA BOOKS
2/3 Hanover Yard, Islington, London N1 8BE

Published in association with the Penguin Group
Penguin Books Ltd, 27 Wrights Lane, London W8 5TZ, England
Viking Penguin, a division of Penguin Books USA Inc.,
375 Hudson Street, New York NY 10014, USA
Penguin Books Australia Ltd, Ringwood, Victoria, Australia
Penguin Books Canada Ltd, 2801 John Street, Markham,
Ontario, Canada L3R 1B4
Penguin Books (NZ) Ltd, 182-190 Wairau Road,
Auckland 10, New Zealand

Penguin Books Ltd, Registered Offices: Harmondsworth, Middlesex,
England

First published in Great Britain by Granta Books 1992
First published in Italy as *La legge degli spazi bianchi*
by Marietti 1989

Printed in England by Butler & Tanner Ltd, Frome and London

ISBN 0-14-014221-5

CONTENTS

PREFACE

Some years ago I resolved to research the lives and careers of a number of doctors I had known when I was a child and had never forgotten. I was in relatively good health at the time, and that fact enabled me to view the individuals with a certain distance, far removed from the terror with which I had regarded them as a boy. (Even for many years afterwards, every visit to the doctor would reawaken in me the old feeling of coming face to face with someone who could determine my fate at his whim.)

My fears were partly dispelled as I studied the contents of the personal archives of Professor S, a history scholar and a man of great intellectual and moral honesty. He had decided, a long time before, to conduct research along the same lines as mine, but with quite a different aim. During our brief conversation seven years ago I was able to establish that for Professor S, medicine, and indeed science in general—notwithstanding the huge advances made in the last few decades—represented 'the darkness born of the light.' I well remember his exact words, as I remember his hasty correction: 'or rather, the light which feeds on the darkness.'

Professor S's voice was very hoarse at the time and I had to strain to hear him. But my discomfort was nothing against the compassion he showed towards those modest doctors who, in the course of their careers, had been forced to try their strength against 'mysteries bigger than themselves.' He had a kind word for all of them, but not for himself. 'They're deciding on my destiny in the Fourth Palace*,' he said with a smile. 'Let's hope they get it over with quickly. What a lot of red tape!'

He lent me the papers relating to the five cases described in this volume. I have summarized them as best I could.

* See 'Treatise on the Palaces', *The Book of Splendours*

THE LAW OF WHITE SPACES

One winter morning Doctor Abraham Fleischmann realized that he could no longer remember the name of his best friend. He was alone in the house; his housekeeper only came in on week-days, and his old friend Lea was confined to her bed with a severe migraine. In the night the doctor had dreamed about an earthquake, and after that about a meeting with a curious individual whose hair shone with brilliantine and whom everyone referred to as the Spirit of the Times. In the morning when he awoke his thoughts turned to his friend, a television announcer and a master of chess.

He had never written down his friend's telephone number in his leather-bound address book, nor stored it in the memory of the personal computer that was a present from his cousin in Connecticut. He phoned his friend every day: it seemed quite unnecessary to commit to paper or to an electronic circuit a series of digits that he had to recall with such frequency. But in November the friend had left for a four-week holiday, and between then and now his telephone number had erased itself from Doctor Fleischmann's memory.

He went to look it up in the telephone directory—but under what name? For more than ten minutes the doctor was unable to recall either the first or the last name of Isaac Rosenwasser. 'I'll just see if I'm still asleep,' he said, pinching his arm. 'Of course, this might be only a dream too,' he went on, aloud. 'Dreaming of pinching oneself—what nonsense,' he thought.

Fleischmann set great store by the discipline, by the almost stately formality of his own thought processes. He was the sort of person who always manages to find a brilliantly appropriate saying for every occasion, and his patients, as well as praising him as a great doctor, considered him a veritable master of life.

In his personal computer he kept a record of every house-call, together with the case history of each and every one of his patients. His emotional life was kept at a safe distance from this attempt to impose a perfect order on the world: neither his mother nor his children, his wife nor his friends had a file on the screen of his computer.

'What is his name?' he persisted to himself that cold morning. 'It's here on the tip of my tongue, and yet I can't remember it. This is ridiculous—we grew up together!'

Before long his indignation turned to fear, timidly at

first, then more violently. 'What if it's the beginning of a disease?' He banished the thought. 'Don't go assuming the worst just because of a simple memory lapse. The synapses of two neurones got a bit mixed up. An ion of sodium or potassium missed the boat between two cells in the cerebral cortex.'

He got out of bed and did a few gymnastic exercises. At fifty-five he was in the prime of life, fit enough on the ski slopes to leave many younger men behind. He had more than one lover among the forward women of the Eighth District, even among the young girls. He telephoned one of them, and during their afternoon encounter in a tiny apartment in Acacia Avenue he was able to forget his disagreeable case of amnesia.

But five days later Doctor Fleischmann was surprised to find himself searching at length and in vain for the word 'injection': the sounds escaped him. He stood speechless before his patient. The word's meaning was circulating in the convolutions of his brain but its sound would not come out. After twenty long seconds the doctor located it again in his acoustic memory. He wrote the patient a prescription for injections of vitamin B12 to be taken once a day for a week.

'I'm so tired!' Fleischmann exclaimed loudly, as soon as the patient had closed the door behind him. 'Perhaps I too ought to take a cure for my nerves. And I must try and put my life back in order. I have too many commitments. I need to sort things out.' At that stage it hadn't occurred to him that he might possibly be dealing with an organic illness. He was sure in himself of the machinery of his body; his daily performances, at sport and in bed, convinced him that it was functioning perfectly.

He wasted no time in attempting to reassure himself that all was well: in an exercise that, while a little childish, was entirely typical of him, he repeated over to himself a hundred times the word 'injection', each time scrutinizing every thought and mental association that passed through his head. In this way he alighted on the thought of death, and beyond it, of nothing. For an instant he felt like he was dying. 'It's obviously a case of an irreversible deterioration of the brain cells,' he thought on the subject of his unexpected amnesia, something that had never occurred to him before then. He began to sweat, and felt an emptiness in his stomach. So, he thought, the pencil was poised over his name; soon it was to be scored off the list of the living. He would end up, limbs rigid, on the marble slab of some dissecting room. And then dissolution, sewage, earth. Was that all there was? Was that what life was about?

Without thinking he made an appointment at a clinic for the next day, and at seven in the morning he went to have blood and urine samples taken. Soon he would know if the machine really was condemned to the scrapyard.

'It's not as if I'm waiting to be sentenced,' he thought as he came out of the clinic. 'The judgement was pronounced long ago, the moment I was cast among the living. It won't matter if one day I can no longer pronounce the word "I", because the "I" will no longer exist, or it will be unable to speak. I won't care.'

He went straight away to see the patients waiting for him. During his visits he noticed with triumphant bitterness and a growing sense of the ridiculous that the number of words disappearing from his vocabulary for seconds, for hours at a time was increasing. It was no longer just words with complicated sounds, like 'plantigrade' or 'clepsydra'; even everyday terms, like 'toothpaste' or 'sand', were beginning to obstruct momentarily the flow of thought in the labyrinth of his brain. 'I'm worse, and deteriorating by the minute,' thought Fleischmann. 'But it will pass. I'll get used to it.'

He went to his wife's house and spent a long time talking with her about trivial, everyday things. He was astonished at how sharp and alert he felt. It was as if he had only begun to live from the moment his life had been put in danger. Before, he'd always seemed to be living in a memory, never in the present, as if he'd been in a larval state, a blind thing, completely bereft of intelligence and consciousness. Now, even his astonishment struck him as an emotion he had never experienced before.

Two days passed in this way. On the third day he went

to get the results of his tests. These revealed a significant alteration in his blood analysis. Three or four values were quite a bit above their normal limits and, in the absence of external intervention, would soon have caused Doctor Fleischmann to have what his colleagues called a Turn. In fact, as he was giving him the results of the tests Flebus asked him, 'Have you had a Turn yet? Do you stammer now and again? Get a bit tongue-tied? Have difficulty getting the words out?' Fleischmann denied that he had. He went home, shut himself in his study and cried.

That evening, in the circle of his former family, with his elbows resting on the clean table-cloth, he looked long and hard at his son, his mother, his wife, all of whom had remained living together after he had moved out. 'Does any of this make sense?' He was coming to realize with a sense of horror that everything he cared most about—love, affection, responsibility for the lives of his dear ones—was deserting him, leaving him in mocking conversation with a world that was a stranger.

'You look pale, Papa,' said his son Benjamin. 'You're taking on too many patients. Perhaps if you wrote fewer prescriptions for purgatives and tried to enjoy life a bit more . . . ' Fleischmann knocked over his bowl of soup and stormed out. As he went he saw a terrified, hunted look on the faces of his wife and son.

Outside in the street near the People's Theatre the evening was cool and full of sounds. The drunks were coming out of the wine cellars on all fours. Fleischmann did not know how to escape his self-inflicted torture. He tried talking some courage into himself. 'Who said the suppositions of science were absolute truths? The human brain is immense: the size of two continents, two planets, two universes. I'll find some way out of this. My time has not yet come.'

He enrolled on a speed reading and memory course that was being held in a dark two-roomed apartment on Joseph II Street.

On the first evening, climbing the blackened staircase of the five-storey building, he met a group of unshaven young people and some fastidious office workers determined to get on in life, all dressed in more or less the same fashion in rough and shoddy clothes. Inside the apartment, on its creaky and worn-out wooden floor, twenty or so chairs and a table were set out in a manner intended to lend a serious and traditional air to the proceedings. This was one of the first private enterprises allowed by the State. 'So the State permits the use of memory!' he thought. 'Quite. The State is all memory. And like all other memories it is destined to destroy itself.'

A few weeks into the course he noticed a significant improvement in his ability to remember names, faces and places of recent acquaintance (remote events had been preserved intact in his memory and in his forgetfulness).

The atmosphere that reigned in the class made him feel as if they were initiates of some sect whose duty was to continue life on earth after the Catastrophe. Reading at speed, across the page, backwards and forwards, up and down, techniques based on the combined use of the senses and on hypnosis; to Fleischmann these were what would sustain him for the rest of his life, what would make it liveable and free from the shame of physical decay. The three weeks of the course were the last bearable moments of the illustrious doctor's existence.

When the course ended he received a diploma and the professor—a small, fair, insignificant-looking man who had learned the techniques of memory in England— heaped praise upon him. Never had he come across a pupil so diligent and at the same time blessed with so much intelligence.

Fleischmann took up his work again full of optimism. He criss-crossed the back streets of the Eighth District, visiting dark apartments and making calls on pensioners with bad hearts and on ninety-year-old women resigned to loneliness. He was full of the conviction that he had something important to offer them: a few minutes of life.

One day returning from his rounds he heard the telephone ring while he was still at the bottom of the stairs. He ran up the remaining steps. He was not in the habit of hurrying, and indeed he hated the phone for the way it enabled the most unforeseen cases of life and death

to reach him, of all people, at any time of the day or night. He hadn't considered that when he had decided to pursue a career in medicine. When he opened the door he found his housekeeper—a thin, deaf eighty-year-old—already holding out the receiver to him with tears in her eyes. 'Come in, come in, Doctor,' whispered the little old lady. 'It's for you.'

This is how Abraham Fleischmann learned of his brother's death. Like him, a doctor, professor of comparative anatomy and a surgeon of international repute, his brother had always had something of a delicate constitution. But his death was a surprise. 'A stroke, or a heart-attack . . . ' Fleischmann murmured to himself with professional objectivity. A moment later he burst into tears, letting out such a painful wail that the old maid fled. The doctor left the house and ran down Kun Street, sobbing loudly and choking on his own tears. A few passers-by turned to stare at him, but left him alone.

Abraham Fleischmann had loved and admired his brother in adulthood. When they were children, however, he had found his brother's melancholy and introspective manner irritating. At that age he wasn't capable of recognizing what gentleness and depth of feeling lay hidden behind his apparent listlessness. Now his brother lay in hospital, wrapped in a sheet like some kind of mummy. He had been dead for half an hour and under the folds of linen Fleischmann could just make out his features, the protrusion of his nose, the shape of his mouth. And though Fleischmann was used to attending to the dead and the dying, the sight had the same effect on him as it has on other men. A cry rose to his lips: 'Why? Why? Why?'

The doctor sobbed and moaned, his face running with tears, while inside he was accusing his brother of being in some way improvident, of having consented to death, of having wanted it. And yet he already knew that, within a few days, he would have yielded to the superior wisdom and mildness of his late brother, whose wish for death— for why else should one so young and so wise have fallen ill?—was simply another expression of his great good sense. To Fleischmann, staying alive now seemed an act of unparalleled foolishness, and the whole of existence nothing more than a huge, filthy, slaughterhouse. He didn't yet know that this single event would within a few days have completely changed the meaning of his life.

The process began suddenly, from the moment he spotted his sister-in-law hiding in a window bay in the hospital corridor. From her he learned that his brother had been ill for a long time, a number of years, and that purely out of regard for his mother—herself suffering from the infirmities of old age—he had hidden the full extent of his illness from everyone, including her.

The day before he died he had summoned all his

strength and telephoned his mother, and when she had asked him how he was, he had told her without hesitation and in a steady voice that he was fine. Then, in the same voice, he had said his goodbyes to her, saying that he was off on a long journey but would be back in a few months. There wasn't a hint of self-pity in his tone. Hanging up the receiver he stared long and hard at the wall before whispering, 'In five or six months' time, once she's got used to my absence, tell her everything. Look after her.'

As he listened to this story, Fleischmann was overcome by a feeling of radiant emotion, as if he were present at some great and solemn event. Then came the moment of truth. First his sister-in-law asked him to go to her house and fetch the clothes to dress the corpse in, telling him in which chest he would find them. There was a short silence. 'Do you still remember the prayer for the dead?' she asked, timidly. 'You have to recite it. If you don't remember it, learn it tonight. It's about twenty lines long. You have to do it. For him. I'm sure you'll manage.'

Doctor Fleischmann left the hospital in great agitation. It was beginning to look as if his brother's fate depended on him, on his ability to learn the prayer for the dead. 'Just now that my memory's in ruins!' he laughed in desperation. 'What nonsense. He's gone and that's that.'

He went to his brother's house, fetched the clothes and took them back to the hospital; then he went to his wife's and mother's house, saying nothing about his brother's death to them, according to the wishes of the deceased, and finally he returned home. He asked his housemaid to find him the old ivory-bound prayer book, its title page covered with the scrawled names of his ancestors and the dates on which they had died.

That evening he didn't eat. He sat down in his dark and dusty study and placed the prayer book in front of him on the writing desk. How long had it been since he had held that book in his hands? Thirty years? Forty? Why did he have to pretend to subscribe to rituals which he had always found childish and incomprehensible? Life and death, the doctor realized, made no more sense to him than those prayers.

He began to wonder what did make sense. The senselessness, the incomprehensibility of everything gripped him like a fever. He felt his ears go red. An almost erotic excitement was taking hold of him. 'No, I won't question it. I know, in the middle of all this uncertainty, that I have to make this small effort, I have to learn these words, these sounds that mean nothing to me. It is the last gift I can give my brother, or my sister-in-law. I, who always held so much back from them.'

He opened the book. At first the square-shaped characters appeared completely unfamiliar to him. The whole system seemed stupidly complicated and arbitrary. 'Still, I don't suppose there's much point in starting to pick holes in the alphabet now that I've made up my mind to go through with it. It's archaic, I know, but right now there's not much of an alternative.'

With the help of a transcription into the Roman alphabet, Fleischmann began to decipher the prayer word by word. But then he decided to memorize the text using the old square characters. Through all this, the meaning of the words remained completely obscure to him. 'It doesn't matter,' he thought, 'even my father who could recite all the prayers so fluently didn't know the meaning of a single word he pronounced. I'll pretend I'm learning a musical score.'

The doctor's thoughts returned to his brother's motionless body, as incontrovertible now in mute self-affirmation as it had ever been in life. And it struck him that the meaning was there, in the self-evidence of a corpse, of an event, the event of death. All the rest—the words, the sounds—merely complicated the significance of such simplicity. But all the same he began to repeat the words over to himself, those useless and necessary sounds, slowly at first, in brief snatches, and then with growing confidence more and more rapidly, lengthening his phrases from three words at a time to seven or eight.

By one in the morning he had said the entire prayer one hundred times over, but still he could remember only the first line. Try as he might, both with the old square characters and with the Roman ones, he was unable to conjure up the remainder before his eyes, nor hear the sounds reverberate in his head. Fleischmann knew from experience how difficult it was to remember sounds for more than a few seconds. His father had been dead only eight years, yet already he had forgotten the sound of his voice. It had become a mere phrase for him, 'a deep, strong voice', no longer a reality. The same would happen with his brother's voice. Even listening to recordings of their voices he would no longer recognize them.

Fleischmann was horrified at the prospect. Following these thoughts, he felt instinctively but obscurely that it was up to him to determine his brother's destiny, even in his present state, deprived of the faculties of memory which sustain the intellect. He began again to repeat the words of the prayer but the telephone rang. It was his sister-in-law asking him to make her something to eat. She had been keeping watch by her husband's bedside and was by now completely exhausted. Her sister had just relieved her. It wasn't right to leave him alone, poor man. She needed a bath and a bite to eat. She would be around in twenty minutes.

'Twenty minutes . . . twenty minutes . . . ' he repeated to himself. Perhaps if they'd left him alone he might have succeeded in learning the rest of the prayer in the remaining hours of the night, but if it went on like this . . . But then how could he deny his sister-in-law the comfort she needed?

'Fine, come on round,' he said, and went to wake the housekeeper. Then, before going to help her prepare a hot meal, he shut himself in his study and tried to see whether the interruption had helped to clear his head and make room in it for a few words of an unknown language. He attempted a quick self-hypnosis, but he was too agitated to use it to help him remember. So he transcribed the text of the prayer into the memory of his personal computer. 'Perhaps tomorrow, reading it over and over on the screen in front of my eyes, I'll learn it. I'll get up at five. No, at half past four.'

His sister-in-law wept copiously, her head bowed over the table. Instead of eating the soup she filled the bowl with the salt tears of her own glands. Long after she had locked herself in the bathroom, Dr Fleischmann could hear her cries. She seemed to be talking to someone, shouting and railing at him, but in the words of a child, blubbered in the sort of secret language that schoolchildren use. It frightened him.

As a child he too used to have conversations, before going to sleep, with someone to whom he only spoke in rhyming verse; and he would ask him every night to let him die together with the rest of his family, all at exactly the same moment, so that none would suffer pain at the death of the others. How long was it since those conversations had ceased? And was it a good thing or a bad thing that they had? 'What a mess we get ourselves into!' he exclaimed, before locking himself in his study.

He spent hours in front of his computer. Until dawn the low hum of the screen was accompanied by a quiet muttering. Then with first light there was silence. At seven in the morning his housekeeper saw him leave the room. 'I've learned it,' the doctor said. He woke his sister-in-law, huddled up on the sofa, with a kiss on the forehead; he took her home for a change of clothes, and together they set out in a taxi for the old cemetery in Kozma Street.

His brother had been washed and dressed and was lying in the simplest of coffins in the House of Purification. His face was a luminous yellow. The terracotta shards placed on his eyes and on his lips made Fleischmann think of a newborn child.

The Purifier of Bodies Goldstein whispered in the cold of the room: 'It took four of us to get him ready. There are four of us. Four, do you understand?' He was looking for an appropriate reward. And as if to demonstrate his own honesty he pulled a wrist-watch out of his pocket. 'Take it. And this was his ring.'

The sheer practicality of this piece of theatre quite distracted Fleischmann from his spasmodic repetition of the prayer for the dead. He gave Goldstein some money, took the objects rescued from an untimely burial, and gave them to his sister-in-law. He unbuttoned his coat, then buttoned it up again; he rubbed his frozen hands together. The Purifier asked him to go outside. 'I bought the grave for both of us,' murmured Fleischmann to his brother as he left, knowing that what he was saying had been heard many times before. 'Goodbye.'

After the speeches, the tears, the brief, thundering prayers, the congregation moved towards the grave. Fleischmann had managed, by paying an appropriate sum, to secure a site near the entrance, away from the older and more overgrown area. A small crowd had gathered, around two hundred people.

The coffin was resting on two planks of wood over the grave. Doctor Fleischmann's heart was beating fast. The time had come for him to recite the prayer for the dead. Someone gently took hold of his arm. He felt a great tension in his chest and in his throat. With a huge effort of will he spoke the first part of the prayer, at the top of his voice, almost shouting it. He had won. The words emerged clearly and distinctly from his mouth, even though for him they were simply sounds without meaning. He, Abraham Fleischmann, was affirming the meaning of the world, of life, beyond all doubt and bitterness. He had to do it for his brother.

He opened his mouth to shout, even louder than before, the second phrase of the prayer for the dead. But with a feeling of terror he realized that he could no longer remember the sounds. The letters themselves had been erased from his memory. He stood gawping, his mouth wide open. The graveyard was silent. Everyone was looking at him. Fleischmann was sure that even his brother was watching him from the coffin. But the second phrase would not come to him. He could only remember one word, one that contained all the vowels, and the mysterious sound of that single word howled around inside his head. Someone understood his embarrassment and spoke the second phrase in his place.

'There, now for the third,' he thought, 'yes, there's that word that reminds me of a dog, yes, like the command to attack. But what might it mean? What is the meaning of that word? I must have someone translate the prayer for me. Maybe then I'll remember it. But no, the meaning doesn't count. It is so vague, so difficult to grasp. It's the form that matters. And it's that—the sounds—that I don't remember any more.'

Someone, meanwhile, was finishing the prayer in a monotonous, sing-song voice, speaking quickly and without reverence. Fleischmann wanted to cling to this word or that as they surfaced from the threatening waves which rose in the lungs of the speaker and headed inexorably towards him.

And then suddenly there was silence. 'Can the prayer have been that short? And I couldn't learn it!'

Someone passed him a shovel. He had to throw the first clod of earth. He bent over, scooped up some earth in the shovel, and threw it on the coffin which had been lowered on ropes into the grave. He heard a thud. It was the sound of the only good deed he had managed to do for his brother.

As some of the crowd scattered and others gathered round him (including his wife and son, alerted by goodness-knows-whom, fortunately without his mother finding out), as he felt himself being shaken by the hand and kissed on the cheeks, Doctor Fleischmann was still trying to evoke the words that he'd found and then lost again.

He returned to work without a period of mourning. What was the point? He had to think of his patients, of his sick, he had to try and help the living since he was unable to help the dead.

And yet every morning after shaving he spent a quarter of an hour repeating the prayer to himself. He brought to bear all the techniques he had learned in the course of the preceding weeks. He used every mental trick he knew, exploited all his psychological skills. He tried to imagine idyllic countryside scenes; he concentrated on regular breathing; he repeated words that were supposed to be able to overcome the guard of what we call consciousness. When he missed a word, he would look at the book. In the evening before going to bed he would switch on the screen, plug in the keyboard and start up the computer for a couple of runs through his act of faith, the prayer for the dead.

After two weeks of this he put himself to the test. Everything went well up to half way through, but his memory of the second part was very poor. He was missing words crucial for their sound or for their graphic impression—their meaning still remained unknown to him. Doctor Fleischmann was taking ten minutes over a prayer which could be spoken in forty seconds.

He continued his efforts, however. 'I won't give up,' he thought. 'I won't give in so easily to illness and degradation.' Fleischmann was convinced that by a supreme exertion of will-power and a faith in his own abilities he would be able to overcome his illness and its symptoms, the loss of short-term memory. Neither techniques nor hypnoses nor computers were of any use; the only thing that could help him was the affirmation of his own existence: 'I am here, I exist!'

His thoughts returned to his brother, silent and motionless in that hospital bed, and to the many sick people he had treated without success. 'They are dead. So they must have been alive. Death is the greatest proof of existence. Forward. I mustn't give up.'

Then one night he had a wonderful dream. He was a king, he was in a golden room, church bells were ringing. He girded on his sword and announced to the people the birth of his son and heir.

He awoke with the same feeling of solemnity in his

veins, in his heart. He went to the hospital and started to work with a will. His patients seemed on their way to recovery, he saw hope for all of them. He continued to repeat to himself the prayer for the dead, but each time he got stuck at the same point, after which he could remember no more. Still he felt he was making progress.

One evening he went to bed exhausted after a long series of visits. He fell asleep and immediately began to dream. In one sense it was the sequel to the dream of a few days before; there was the solemn air of a momentous event.

He was in a beautiful room; his brother entered, looking healthy, elegant, a little awkward the way he had always been, and stopped in front of him. He reached out towards the doctor, incredibly happy and benevolent; then laid his hand on his shoulder and began to recite word for word the prayer for the dead. He smiled as he pronounced the meaningless syllables. But this time it seemed to the doctor, quite unexpectedly, that he understood their meaning. There was no need to translate the words, the sounds, into this or that language; they had a sense—inexplicable, unrepeatable—in themselves.

Fleischmann kissed his brother's hands as he continued his serene psalmody. And then something else became clear: all the childish meanings that the doctor had attributed to the words—because of the resemblance of some sounds to those of words he knew—really were there; they seemed to coexist happily with the real and solemn meanings and they cheered his spirits. From time to time an obscenity would jump out of that dance of syllables and sounds, and it too would be joyful, not offensive.

When his brother had finished saying the last word of the prayer, Doctor Fleischmann said to himself in his dream: 'At last I've learned the whole thing. For it was I who was reciting the prayer. My brother was just a figure in my dream. So I can't be ill. The worst of the sentences that nature can pass, the biochemical disturbances by which fats paralyse and obscure our blood vessels, count for nothing. For man exists beyond memory, beyond language and meaning.' He was already half awake before he had finished this sentence.

He opened his eyes and saw the grey light of early morning. His feeling of joy evaporated instantly. 'What if it really was my brother who said the prayer from start to finish? Perhaps he really did visit me, who knows how, who knows from where?'

He was deeply moved and began to cry. 'I can't do a good deed for my dead brother, but he, dead as he is, can do one for me! We're not alone on the earth, we're not alone. There is an infinite host of beings who love us, as my brother knew how to love, and who intervene for our sake inside us. I would never have believed it was possible.' And in his turn he thought of his brother with that feeling of belated love that can remain a torment a whole life long.

The telephone rang and the doctor was called to help a poor old woman of seventy-five who had had a heart attack. He dressed in a hurry saying only to his maid: 'She won't die. I'm sure of it.'

He went out and ran all the way from Karfenstein Street to Danko Street. He tried, breathless from running, to recite the prayer just to be sure. He was unable to remember a single syllable. He stopped. He wanted to batter his head against the wall. 'No. I mustn't give up. My brother will help me again. He'll help me every time I need him.'

When he arrived at Mrs Wolf's house she had been dead for a few minutes. The doctor stood looking at the corpse as he had looked at many before in his long experience in medicine. 'With her last words she thanked you, Doctor,' a relative said. 'This corpse thanked me,' Fleischmann thought. He stared at it for a while, then left the house without signing the death certificate.

After those of the prayer, other words began to disappear little by little from Doctor Fleischmann's vocabulary. Faces and shapes disappeared from his sight, melodies from his hearing. Towards the end his memory had almost completely deserted him. When they took him in to St John's Hospital, he didn't remember ever having had a brother. To Isaac Rosenwasser, who together with a nurse helped him into the ambulance, he said: 'Everything is written in the white spaces between one letter and the next. The rest doesn't count.' Among his notebook pages of appointments and scientific observations, on the back of an instruction sheet for the use of his computer, was the following scrawl: 'The louder you shout, the better he'll hear you.'

For the complete works of A. Fleischmann, see *New Life*, nos 1, 2, 3, 4, 1970

A.R. Luria, *A Prodigious Memory*, Moscow, 1968

A.R. Luria, *A World Lost and Found*, Moscow, 1971

THE CLOCK OF LIFE

Don't be shocked, dear brother, by the case I'm about to lay before you; don't be ashamed or disgusted or scandalized, I beg you, by what you are about to learn. You know me as well as you know yourself; and though things can turn out an infinite number of different ways, and the natural order has been taking knocks ever since man appeared on the earth, you know what to expect of me.

Your research into what you call the 'biological clock' has convinced you that life is made up of a string of physical processes and chemical reactions whose sequence is rigidly fixed—within certain more or less predictable limits—in time and space and follows predetermined patterns. I'm sorry to say that my own experience, much as it may disgust you, stands in absolute contradiction to your conception of existence. I say all this ironically, in self-doubt and desperation, and with the distressing vagueness that accompanies a state of alcoholic delirium.

41

I know exactly how you see it: we are simply machines made of matter, with all the attendant faults one would expect. But there is another possibility, one we hear so little about. If we take it into consideration it can give our lives meaning, or make them incomprehensible. And that's why I'm writing to you, to tell you about this possibility, and about my own case. From here, where I've been living in hiding for three years, from this miserable refuge I can bear witness with my own life to the strangeness of an existence which—whether seen from the vicinity of someone who is involved, or from an infinite distance—gives the lie to every one of nature's laws, known or merely guessed at.

What of me? Some years ago my destiny took such a strange and unexpected turn for the worse that I've thought it better to break off all contact with friends and acquaintances of old, with professional colleagues and even with those closest to me, such as you, dear brother. But today I've decided to let you know I'm alive and to confront you with the difficult subject of my existence. If you want you can seek me out. Otherwise I'll live out the rest of my days in happy degradation—but who can judge these things?—without ever again attempting to rejoin the society of other people.

You know how committed I was to my vocation as a doctor, with what patience and perseverance I tried to keep faith with my charges in our derelict neighbourhood, where I've always worked, a neighbourhood of abandoned old people and hopeless drunks. These specimens of humanity demand the most care and the greatest understanding from a doctor with a conscience. It is here that the cry is weakest and the heartbeat is most faint. My story must begin with one of these pitiful cases. Of course I want to take a little time before telling you about me, but I also want to try and make you understand how much I was influenced by your research.

I was on my way to Danko Street one day to visit an old woman of ninety. Crossing the market I was struck by the sound of the calls of the hawkers and street-traders. I listened more closely: I wanted to hear all the individual voices; to take pleasure in them all at once, and in each distinct from the others. And at the same time it occurred to me how much invisible activity—of molecules, of chains of acids and proteins—went to make up the organisms running around and making all this noise. If only one were capable of hearing those sounds, the consonances and dissonances of chemical compounds as they bonded, broke apart and transformed themselves! I'm telling you this because the old lady I was on my way to see, a tiny woman but quite alert and full of energy, had a very strong heart—I had known this for years and years—which affirmed with every beat all the will to live of an organism that was not yet ready to break down into its constituent elements.

Each time I went to see her I was filled with a sense of happiness. I would check her blood pressure, her appetite and her digestive function; that was all she needed. And on every visit I was reminded of your own fascinating field of study: the clock that regulates all our lives and also—should a chain of fats obstruct some chemical reaction, a poison destroy some vital function, or simply if the clockwork runs down—leads inexorably to death. But why is it that the clockwork, for want of another word, has to run down? This was the question that occurred to me that day as I arrived at the house of my elderly patient, Mrs Hirsch.

Climbing the dirty, blackened stairs of the three storey building on the corner of Danko Street and Wednesday Street I took out of my case the little bag of toffees I always brought the old lady. Thirty years before her only son had gone to live in a distant continent and she had no other surviving relatives. Her son did come to visit her once a year however. For a week he would drag her along to cafés and theatres, buy her dresses and shoes— which she never wore—then leave again. Mrs Hirsch lived for that week, and had been doing so now for thirty years. She had never been to visit her son, 'so as not to be a burden on him.'

Arriving on the landing I found the door of my patient's apartment slightly ajar. I knocked, pushed the door open and went in. The only window in the small

44

single room was shut, the curtains drawn. Seated in her armchair in those darkened surroundings, Mrs Hirsch seemed to give off a certain luminosity. She was dead. I could tell that she must have passed away some time in the night. The pain I felt at the death of my charge was redoubled by a tremendous pang of guilty remorse. Out of sheer carelessness I had not been to see her for nearly a fortnight, and I felt that this omission might somehow have been the cause of the old lady's death.

I asked myself again and again why it was that her small light, without which the world now seemed so dark, had had to go out. Was it because I had not fed her with the love that her delicate state demanded of me? Or was it for some other reason? I was filled with self-reproach. I was even on the point of resigning my post as district doctor and retiring to some position in the office of public health.

I was the one who paid the funeral expenses—the old dear had left me all her possessions and savings in her will—and who bought the grave. And this was how the death of Mrs Hirsch took on for me all the aspects of a prodigious event of rare and solemn justice. For as I was arranging transport for the coffin, I came across a telegram which had arrived from Canada on the very day of her death, informing Mrs Hirsch of the 'tragic loss' of her son Benjamin two days before. I found out later, in a letter from an acquaintance of the deceased, that he had died without warning, of a heart attack.

And now perhaps you will begin to understand the strange fascination your research has for me: the way in which the clock of life sometimes stops for reasons that are as mysterious as they are impartial, and often informed by a unique sense of mercy. For you must know that by comparing the precise times of death I was able to ascertain that Mrs Hirsch preceded her son to the grave. Chance—if that's what you like to call it—had been extraordinarily kind to that old lady, deserted and alone in her old age. The heart attack, the 'kiss of death', had spared my patient terrible suffering. Or else the spring which regulated the clockwork of the son in exile led beyond his body to a bond which not even the distance between two continents could break. What is this bond? The workings of some hormone secreted by the hypothalamus? Are these chains of acids so potent that they can cross mountains and oceans and deserts?

And it was during that period, while I was still troubled by these momentous events, that I had the encounter which would bring about a sea-change in my life. I was still overwhelmed by intense feelings of excitement and despondency when I was called out on a visit to the old apartment building where we used to live. Do you remember it? The yellow tiles in the courtyard, the black enamelled wrought iron railings, the ramshackle old elevator all welcomed me with the same harsh indifference that I felt every day on my way home from school. I had been very unhappy in that building. Now, with a scientist's detachment, I can ascribe my oppressed childhood and my unhappy adolescence to various factors: genetic, psychological, environmental, and so on. But the unhappiness that I felt there seemed greater than even the sum of all these various internal and external factors. Having said that, I don't feel particularly depressed about it today; on the contrary, I feel strangely light-headed. And of course I should add that there was always the sight of Adele Polak to lighten up those dark days I spoke of.

Every afternoon from June to September she would sit down on her doorstep to sunbathe. Our house was deserted; we used to watch her secretly, pushing aside the net curtain on the kitchen door which opened onto the railed courtyard. Do you remember Mrs Polak? She would have been about thirty or thirty-five then. She nearly always appeared in shorts, lying in a deck-chair, her legs stretched out in front of her. Her skin was smooth and shiny, and the sun seemed to join in her splendour. I think I might even have written a poem about her one time. Every day I waited, my heart in my mouth, for her to appear. She lived on the other side of the courtyard, one floor higher than us.

When the nurse gave me the address it didn't occur to me to think of her, nor was I particularly surprised or moved when she came to the door. 'Help me, Doctor, please. I've heard so many good things about you. It's such a long time since we've seen each other. I watched you grow up. Please help me. My husband is so ill.' A door opened in the dark hall and the husband came towards me. It all seemed perfectly natural, as if everything had continued exactly as it had once been, without interruption; as if no time had passed. I had no trouble recognizing the man I had last seen thirty years before; he looked almost exactly as I remembered him, even though he was now nearly eighty years old. Only his voice turned out to be quite foreign to me; it was raw and cracked, inhuman somehow. Compared to the wrinkles which had invaded the features of his face, the distortion of his voice seemed to owe more to some cruel and distant cause. He muttered something incomprehensible then turned and opened the door he had just closed behind him. Only then did I become aware of the stench in the place. I could see into a darkened room lit only by a red lamp on a little table covered with old lace. I was shown in, Mrs Polak was leaning lightly on my arm. I looked her in the face for the first time since I had entered that awful place. I immediately noticed her teeth: they were intact, a little yellowed, but still with that gap between the two central incisors that gave her, even as a grown woman, the look of a little girl. And although almost seventy years old, she still had the smile that had entranced me thirty years before.

'He doesn't remember a thing,' Adele Polak whispered, leading me into the room. 'Not even what he told me a minute ago. It's terrible.' We took our seats. Adam Polak sat down opposite me in a velvet-covered armchair. He stared at me with eyes that had lost none of their melanin content; they were darker than those of a young man, but lifeless. I realized that it was extremely difficult to communicate with him. Whatever I said to him he would have forgotten a moment later, and I would be lost for an explanation.

I opened the old bag father gave me on my graduation and took out the stethoscope to listen to his breathing and his heartbeat. His lungs fluttered timidly. After a little I stopped listening and looked at him. His hair, smooth, shining and dyed black, gave him the look of a waxwork. I took out my sphygmomanometer to take his blood pressure, a routine measure. 'Put it away!' yelled the old man. 'Put it away or I'll break it! You're not going to kill me with your machines! Just watch out!'

I was dealing with a hopeless case. I should have had him hospitalized there and then, and for good. His wife's large brown eyes were begging me to. She was blushing, something you encounter only rarely in someone of that age: she was red-faced with shame. But we know, dear brother, what really lies behind feeling shy, feeling ashamed, blushing, do we not? It hides something which cannot be confessed in words: not repentance, reluctance or the wish to remain hidden, but rather the opposite.

I rose, disturbed, to take my leave, giving Adele a prescription for a mild sedative. 'Who are you?' asked the old man, this time without aggression.

'I am a doctor. I'm here to make you well again.'

'Impossible,' he shouted. Then, calm once again, he turned to his wife: 'Is he here with my death certificate?'

I fled from the room, from that ruined life. Adele came with me, closed the door behind her, and suddenly in the darkened hallway burst into stifled sobs.

'Rescue me, rescue me, I beg you. I've always been fond of you. It's so difficult to find someone you can trust, someone to confide in. Men always die on you. Won't you help me?' She leaned on my shoulders and kissed my cheeks. She was wearing perfume. Even her dress, red with white flowers, gave out a faint, girlish scent. 'I've nobody left, all my relations are dead. Illness is a terrible thing; all the evil, all the spite comes out. Save me!'

I promised her that the very next day I would make arrangements for her husband to be admitted to a psychiatric ward. 'There's no remission from his illness, at least from what we know today.' The old man's brain was obviously riddled with disease.

'I'm afraid that he'll attack me in the night. I've found him twice with a knife hidden under the pillow. Can I call you if he gets worse during the night?' I promised her that

I would certainly come if it was necessary, she only had to telephone. 'He doesn't seem dangerous to me. He hasn't reached that stage. Try to do as he says,' I suggested to her. I pulled myself from her embrace and ran off.

That night I didn't shut my eyes. I kept thinking of Adele Polak and her husband. I fell asleep with the image of them in the prime of life, not yet grown old and driven insane by illness. How had such a change in fortunes come about? With their business as second-hand dealers they had amassed great wealth. I lay thinking, half-awake and half-asleep, of all the old people, helpless and half-mad as they were now, that they must have swindled out of furniture, clothes, shoes, the last tokens of their existence, in exchange for next to nothing. That was when they hadn't actually been paid for clearing a house of all its junk, leaving it as empty as a shell. Now it was their turn. But perhaps Adele Polak had not been quite as cruel as her husband, I thought. I was reluctant to accept the idea that the woman of my youth was capable of taking part in such exploitation. Sinking into sleep I saw her again in her shorts. She was in the courtyard, crying in heart-rending sobs.

I awoke with a start and without thinking began to dress. It was two in the morning. I was terrified by the thought of finding her already dead. I ran to the corner of Strand Road and rang for the concierge. I had been called by the Polaks, I stammered. Taking the old elevator, I caught a glimpse of the concierge's vacant look as I closed the door. As I arrived at the fifth floor I saw a door opening slowly. Mrs Polak was waiting for me.

'Thank you, thank you, I was sure you'd come. It is really kind of you. I was so frightened. He's had a terrible attack. He's sleeping now. I don't know what I'd have done without you.'

She showed me into the kitchen, switched on the light, put the cafetière on the stove and switched the light out again, leaving only the gas flame to illuminate the room. 'This way they won't see us through the curtains. They could see our shadows.' She stayed by the stove, but turned towards me. 'When you were a boy you really loved me and wanted me. But I knew you'd soon forget me, and that's why I didn't return your feelings. You could have had me easily you know. Now you've become a man, your greying hair makes you even more attractive. I love you. You see the clock of our lives has always run fast or slow, but never kept time for us. And now here we are, brought together by suffering.'

What did she know of me, of my feelings, of time, and of its measure? 'I don't know what you mean, Mrs Polak. I only came to . . . '

'Don't say anything! That's a lot of lies.' She sat down next to me, on the same seat, and took my hands. 'We can still live together, we can try. I know you still want me. It wouldn't be the first time in history. I've always thought of you, all these years. Time isn't really like I said it was just now . . . fast or slow, it doesn't matter. We have to find each other.'

There was something provocative in her look, in her expression. I thought then that the agent of whatever illness had destroyed her husband's mind might also exist in her. I promised her that I would think about what she had said and that to be on the safe side I would call the ambulance in the morning to take Mr Polak away. She calmed down, moved away from me and poured the coffee made with yesterday's grounds. I recalled the neighbourhood gossip that her husband had accumulated a considerable fortune thanks as much to his legendary meanness as to his professional abilities.

'We could be happy. Think about it. Everything I have will be yours. We'll go and live in another part of town where nobody knows us. Please . . . please.' She kissed me on the lips. I was aware of her warmth and her perfume, and something so lewd that I drew back in alarm. I made my excuses, saying that I had another call to make.

'I know that isn't true. But go anyway. Think of it till tomorrow, I beg you. Look at me. Promise you'll come back. I'll make you come back anyhow, like I made you come tonight.'

Was I simply acting according to her plan? I became angry. But Adele's eyes filled with tears, and at the same time she smiled a bitter smile, her lips creased, the smile of a passionate, disillusioned woman. She kissed my hands, and I caressed the back of her neck. I felt sorry for her. She opened the door without another word. The concierge asked after Mr Polak and I told him all was well.

Two days later I learned from a patient that Adam Polak and his wife had died that night, suffocated by gas. A neighbour, alerted by the smell, had smashed the glass in the door and discovered their two bodies locked in an embrace. For many nights I dreamed of those two unhappy people, the petrified face of old Adam Polak and the cheerful expression, the sensual mouth, the pretty hands of his wife. I was seized by an overwhelming longing for her: for her bitter-sweet voice, for her hands as they caressed me that night, for the scent of her dyed hair, for her silk dress. My desire tormented me no less than my remorse. What had happened to the molecules of my body? Had my olfactory receptors and my centres of vision undergone some structural change that they were now reliving the stimuli they had first perceived thirty years ago, rather than those of the present? Had my entire central nervous system turned itself upside-down? Or does the clock of life run in such a way that defies understanding? I knew I could easily have accepted the love that poor Adele Polak proffered that night, and in doing so would either have confirmed or corrected a fault in the mechanism. But perhaps the mechanism is capable

54

of producing only errors, and these have been perpetuated in the combining and recombining of acids since the formation of the first living molecule. Life itself might be due to such an error.

Faced with those two deaths, faced with total uncertainty about the meaning of it all, I found no better resort than that most ancient expression of desolation: drunkenness. Naturally after a short time I had to give up my job; I began to steal, I ended up in prison a few times, and in the asylum. Now I'm an alcoholic.

You can meet me in the market where you'll find me sweeping up the dirt, moving boxes and wooden cases around. I often talk to myself. I often hear whispering behind my back: 'He used to be a doctor, well-bred, a man of culture. Ending up like this. What a shame!' Every evening as I throw myself down on my bed of cardboard boxes I think of my love and of the injustice of it all. It hurts terribly. I hope it will end soon.

(This was Dr Spitzer's last letter. Don't ask what happened before or after, if you don't want the 'before' and 'after' to collide in your head.)

K. Spitzer, *The Operon Circuit in the Control of Gene Action*, Colorado, 1970

J. Monod and F. Jacob, 'Teleonomic Mechanisms in Cellular Metabolism', *Cold Spring Harbour Symposia*, 1961

VERA

Schekkinah is what our holy sages call that part of God's being in which the light has grown weak in order to allow the angels and the souls to exist.

J. d. P.

And for that reason Schekkinah would sooner permit invading demons to injure her with sharp spears than obstruct man's everlasting happiness.

The Book of Splendours

I'll never forget the case I came across recently in a little country in Central Europe where I was stationed from the first days of the armistice. My duty was to organize aid to the starving population of one of the tiny states in the area, in Hungary, and I was sent from Berlin with a cargo of food, medicine, blankets and toothbrushes.

The aid parcels were distributed in old cinemas, ruined school halls and bombed theatres to silent crowds of evil-smelling people who tore them from our hands. One day about a month ago, from the stage of an old theatre, I spotted a woman coming towards us. She was not alone . . .

They came towards the doctor slowly, the woman holding the child from behind. With each step the woman took, the child's legs moved like a marionette's. She walked as if pushed along by the belly of her older companion who was holding her under the arms. A blue handkerchief covered her hair, emphasizing the perfect regularity of her features and the innocence of her expression. The woman standing behind her had olive skin and large eyes set in deep sockets; she looked like a model for what the child would become three decades later.

'How old is the little one?' asked the doctor, as the exaggeratedly swaying steps came to a stop in front of him. He placed his hand gently on the sick child's neck.

The woman did not reply. A smile broke out between her large, irregular teeth.

'Six or seven, I suppose,' the doctor continued, smiling back. The child nuzzled him in the stomach, rubbing her nose in his coat. He moved away without appearing to be shocked.

'Dear child, you mustn't do that,' he murmured, his smile widening.

'The child is sixteen years old,' her mother said suddenly, more as if she wanted to clarify matters than to contradict him.

Doctor Friedmann took a step back. 'Good God,' he thought, 'sixteen! That's impossible. The woman's mad. The child's obviously not a dwarf. Still there's no way she can be sixteen and look like that. But what if the mother—it must be her mother—what if she isn't mad? How could she joke about something so serious? How could a mother's heart be so indifferent? But the child is clearly having great difficulty in walking. Perhaps she's suffered the scourge of polio?'

All of this happened a long time ago, when the planet was still plagued by awful diseases, by now all but eradicated.

'Would you let her go for a minute?' said the doctor, and the woman, after a moment's hesitation, removed her arms encircling the child's chest. But she didn't move far away, standing ready to catch her if she fell. The tiny body began to sway, but the head remained straight and erect. And at that moment the child's eyes, which until then had been firmly closed, flew open wide. She stared at the doctor with a look completely devoid of intention and significance, irresistible in its neutrality. The man felt himself being sucked into her gaze. Again he took a step backwards.

'What lies behind those eyes?' he wondered, lowering his head, unable to withstand the force of a stare which drew everything towards a single point—the centre of her consciousness—where nothing seemed to exist.

'She has had three operations on her brain. She was treated by Professor Olivecrona in Sweden. That's where our inheritance went—the rest was taken by the war. My husband, my parents, my brothers and sisters, they're all dead. There are only the two of us left alive.'

The woman said all of this quietly but without reticence. A long silence followed. The child closed her eyes and the doctor, sensing the force of her stare fade, worked up the courage to look at her again.

The blue handkerchief hinted at a beautifully shaped head, fine and gracefully rounded. Her face, devoid of sharp angles and tinged with pink around the cheek bones, seemed perfectly complete in itself. Her small straight nose, her soft pink lips, fleshy without being aggressive and with a soft but precise outline, could not have been other than they were.

'I've never seen anything more beautiful,' thought the doctor. Looking at this small creature, the picture of innocence, he was deeply moved. She was wearing a red dress with white flowers, and little red canvas shoes. Her breathing was but the slightest murmur, gentle and perfumed, and so unobtrusive that it excited admiration rather than pity.

'What's your name?' the doctor asked, almost whispering so as not to break the spell.

The child neither moved nor opened her eyes.

'Her name is Vera,' her mother answered for her. 'She hasn't spoken a single word for three years.'

Vera. The name sounded so false, so deliberate, that the doctor began to doubt the whole thing.

'Is she really as old as you said before?' The woman nodded her head in confirmation, her eyes fixed on the doctor. A succession of differing expressions passed rapidly across her face, in complete contrast to her daughter's. The doctor took note of the relatively young appearance of the mother. He guessed she was about thirty-five. Her slim, supple body showed off its well formed curves under a light and elegant dress of shiny green silk.

'What can they possibly want from us?' the doctor asked himself again. 'They are not reduced to misery, like these others. The war seems barely to have touched them. Perhaps they've simply come for the aid packages.'

Looking up, he saw the ragged crowd, the inhabitants of that ruined district who had survived the slaughter of war. They stood there in the empty stalls of a theatre whose stage was piled up with parcels from all over the world. The theatre seats had probably ended up as fuel in the neighbours' stoves. The end-of-May sun filtered through the wide open doors.

'Does she have the medicines she needs? Might I be able to help find them?' the doctor asked.

'I don't need medicine. The child is perfectly healthy. We came for the aid parcels. What is in them?'

The man signalled to two soldiers who were wearing white silk armbands bearing the symbol of the red cross. The soldiers took from the pile two small parcels made of rough packing cardboard. They gave them to the woman.

'There. Have a look for yourself,' the doctor murmured, not lifting his gaze from two of the strangest individuals he had ever met. The woman opened one of the packs, glanced indifferently at the contents and said: 'Wonderful. I'm sure it will all be very good.'

She put the parcels in a string bag she carried on her arm.

'For all eventualities, since your case is so out of the ordinary, would you like to leave us your address? Perhaps later we might be able to be of some help to you.'

'My address?' The woman looked blank for a moment as she repeated the word. Finally she whispered: 'Grand Transport Street, number 24.'

The doctor took down the address in the margin of the list of names he was holding. Then the woman and the child did an about-turn pivoting on the little girl's left leg. Darkness and the silent crowd of starving people soon hid the two figures from the doctor's sight.

That night Friedmann could get no peace. He tossed and turned from side to side, prey to an inexplicable anxiety. Sudden wild racings of his heart alternated with long bouts of feeling faint. Around five in the morning the doctor finally fell asleep, exhausted, lying flat on his back.

The next day he didn't go to the Communal Theatre. He brushed his uniform, took his doctor's bag and set out to look for Grand Transport Street.

He had difficulty finding it, despite the accuracy of the

map headquarters had supplied. Many of the houses had been destroyed and in some places the street signs—small white painted metal plates bearing the names of the streets in black—were missing. Majestic buildings stood exposed, disintegrating quietly.

Doctor Friedmann looked up with a start. One storey up, from the mullioned window of a neo-Gothic apartment building, the child's mother was waving at him, beckoning him up.

He skirted around what looked like a bomb crater, crossed the road and went into the greenish-stuccoed five-storey building.

He found himself in a long low passage. A gold-lacquered plaster statue of a boy admiring himself in the mirror graced the stairwell. At the top of the first flight he came face to face with the woman, who was smiling behind her deep-set eyes.

'It was quite by chance I saw you,' she said, waiting on the stairs. 'I rarely look out of the window.'

'I was lucky,' replied the doctor.

'Lucky?'

'Yes. I really wanted to see you. In any case I had your address.'

How had he let such a compromising admission slip out? The doctor was shocked to find himself standing there like a beggar, no longer the just father handing out rewards and punishments, cures and illnesses, even death itself.

'I thought you were just passing; I wanted you to have a look at the child. She has a bit of a cough. I'm the one who is in luck: it's so hard to find a doctor these days, and I would have had to take the child with me. You know how difficult it is. The telephone lines are still not working.'

But in spite of what she had just said the woman did not move from her position, as if to prevent the doctor coming any further up the stairs.

'I have to confess that I came here with the sole purpose of seeing you. It was no accident that you saw me from your window.' As he was saying this, Friedmann was aware that he was obeying a strange uncontrollable impulse.

A faint, hoarse cry sounded unmistakably from the landing: 'Mama, ma-ma.' The child was wearing a pink cotton dress and a pale red headscarf decorated with white butterflies. The doctor leaned back against the wall.

'Good God, the child can talk!'

'She says one word every five or six days. Always the same: mama. She doesn't know any others. She might not even know that I am her mother, that I gave birth to her. Perhaps she just repeats the sound because it corresponds to something she's heard, maybe from me,' the woman muttered, half to herself. 'Come on, let's not leave her alone. She might fall over. Every so often she has a fit.'

'Epilepsy?'

'Yes. She just collapses without any warning, and hurts herself. One of her teeth is loose. The next time she might knock it out.'

'Don't let her fall,' yelled the doctor. 'Don't leave her for an instant.'

Inside the house everything was immaculate, as if the war had passed the rooms by. The walls, decorated with great purple flowers outlined in gold on a silver background, were perfectly intact. The living room was filled with elegant bentwood furniture. Glass-fronted cabinets displayed porcelain figurines. The woman sat the child down in an armchair upholstered in red velvet and indicated a sofa to the doctor.

'We would rather have suffered the cold of winter than sell a single stool, a single chair. My father collected examples of Viennese furniture. My family were all very sensitive, they loved Vera so much. Do you remember, little one, how grandmother would take your hand and sing to you? You know, don't you, that grandmother is gone?'

The child's mouth and eyes took on a hardly perceptible expression, the merest hint of a smile.

'You see how she smiles?' said her mother. 'If you can see that, it means you understand her, you understand people, life. If you can't . . . '

The man looked hard at the child and he imagined he

could see what the woman was describing.

'I knew immediately that you were a good person, gentle and caring. I noticed from the start your concern for the child. That's why I called you here.'

'You called me here?'

'Yes, with my thoughts.' As she was saying this the woman sat down next to the doctor. 'It always works like this!'

I've fallen into the clutches of a madwoman, he thought.

He felt something brush against the back of his hand, light and somewhat irritating, like the legs of an insect. The instant he pulled back his arm he became aware of Vera's tiny form standing in front of him, her arm stretched out towards him as if to stroke him. But he knew almost immediately that he must have imagined this, since all he could actually see was the brusque withdrawal of his own arm, an absurd twitch, and the effect his violent movement had on the child. All of a sudden her expression changed to one of blank, ashen-faced stupor; he caught a flash of white teeth between her lips before her small body crowned with white butterflies fell to the floor with a dull thud.

'Good God, her tooth!' Seizing the child by the wrist and supporting the nape of her neck with her other hand, the mother began to wail. The child's body was stretched rigid, jerking and twitching to the electric impulses of the epileptic convulsions.

'Help me, please. We must carry her over there. Please.'

The doctor leaped to his feet, pressed the child's hand in his own, and held it till the convulsions became less violent and finally stopped altogether. Then stroking Vera's smooth round face he began to murmur words of tenderness, the most tender words he could find in himself to say. He hadn't spoken like that for decades. He picked the child up, one arm behind her knees, the other supporting her shoulders and waited for her mother to show him where to take her.

They came into a darkened room where a huge white bed blotted out nearly all of his field of vision. Beyond, a door opened into another room lit by the reddish light of an oil lamp.

'Come in,' said the woman, returning with the lamp and lighting the way to the smaller room. Once inside, Friedmann noticed that it was filled with dolls and toys of every sort. 'Be careful you don't trip up.' The woman's voice was still thick with tears. He felt paralysed with trepidation.

He walked towards that tabernacle carrying the child's body with all the respect due to the Scrolls of the Law. He remembered carrying his own son like that after he had twisted his ankle on a trip—how time had flown by!—through the Rocky Mountains.

The seven-year-old boy, jumping down on to the path, had dared to defy nature and the limits of his own body. Now, at twenty-five, he could boast a real talent for mathematics, for music, and his marks in theology were evidence of a rare depth of intellect.

'Put her down here, gently. Gently, I beg you.' The woman was nearly invisible in her dark blue dress. She smoothed the pillow and waited for the doctor to lay the tiny body down in the white child's cot. She began to take off the child's clothes and the man instinctively turned to withdraw to the adjoining room.

'Don't go . . . ' said the woman, drawing one corner of her mouth into a half-smile. Vera's snow-white skin was revealed, her breasts half the size of a fist, the swelling of her belly, her sparse covering of pubic hair, her straight, tapering legs.

'Have you ever seen such a perfect body? Who knows who she takes it from. Not from me, as you yourself can see.'

The mother smiled again and with great difficulty helped the child into her nightdress. The next moment Vera fell back on to the pillow and closed her eyes as if she wanted to sleep.

He was suddenly aware of a strong perfume which seemed to emanate from the mother and the child. 'Rêve d'Or,' he thought, 'I'd know it anywhere. The girls at school used to wear it.'

'It's always like that,' said the mother. 'She reacts to any strong external stimulus by having a fit. It is probably not your fault, Doctor, that she fell over just now. I don't think you had anything to do with it. You just gave her a little push and the child reacted badly to it.'

'How can I make amends? I was too brusque with her. One has to be so careful in a case like this.'

'Don't blame yourself. I'd rather you gave me a hand.' The woman's face tightened. 'I'm going to open her mouth. You will see her broken tooth. Help me pull it out.'

He started. 'No, please. Let's wait till tomorrow and find a dentist.'

'Out of the question. Can't you see it's bleeding?'

A thin trickle of blood oozed from the left corner of Vera's mouth.

'Come,' she said, in a tone which brooked no argument. 'You hold her arms and legs and I'll pull out the tooth.'

He did as he was told, powerless to resist. He approached the bed and held the child down, using his hands and the weight of his body. The woman took hold of the scarf which covered Vera's head and with a sharp tug pulled it away. Her small head, like a new-born child's crowned with a few very fine hairs, brought home to the doctor the fragility of her condition.

'Her hair has stopped growing. Three years ago we had

a wig made for her, but I haven't made her wear it for a few months. What's the point? Now hold tight . . . '

The mother parted Vera's bloody lips with her finger and took hold of the broken incisor which hung wretchedly from her gum. She wound one corner of the scarf around it. A hoarse cry emerged from the girl's throat. The mother yanked hard on the free corner of the scarf and pulled out the tooth.

The next moment she was sitting on the sofa, sobbing miserably. 'Why, why does it have to be like this? What will become of the poor child?'

The man was filled with a terrible sense of despair. He let the child go, wiped the blood from her mouth and turned to her mother. He sat down beside her and put his arm around her shoulders.

'You have to hope for the best,' he murmured, kissing her tear-stained cheeks. 'Hope for the best.' The woman pressed against him.

That night Abraham Friedmann had a strange dream, from which he awoke with a start at four in the morning. He felt the need to get in touch immediately with the woman he had dreamed about. He dressed in haste and went out into the street, convinced that the dream had revealed to him the future course of his existence. He felt unusually happy and surprised himself by skipping through the moonlit ruins. But he could also see the first grey light of dawn.

The people he met on the way depressed him. Tramps and vagrants stretched out on the ground, immersed in an unjust sleep; some old man raving; the elderly prostitutes clicking their heels as they walked up and down with their net bags in their hands; all gave him the impression that nothing had changed with the new day.

'I was coming to see you,' murmured the woman, appearing out of nowhere just two steps away from him.

'What are you doing here?' Friedmann asked, almost breathless with shock.

'I was coming to see you. I couldn't stand the idea of not seeing you for so long.'

'And what about the child, did you leave her alone?'

'Yes, I tucked her in so she can't get out of bed.'

The doctor's good mood changed to one of panic. 'You can't do that—it's dangerous! Have you ever done it before?'

'No, this is the first time. But I just couldn't bear the idea of you being so far away. They might transfer you tomorrow to another city and then what would become of us?'

The doctor didn't dare ask who she meant by 'us', whether it was her and him or her and the child. He took her arm and they set off in a hurry for Grand Transport Street.

'Who knows where this might lead?' he thought. 'It's a dangerous business, getting involved with a woman. After the first time they want your soul. I don't even know whether I should tell her about my dream.' But he hadn't gone five hundred yards with her along the way before he was seized by an irresistible impulse to tell her everything. Against his better judgement, and becoming more breathless by the second, he began to recount his dream.

The woman might not have been listening. She opened the heavy outer door, left unlocked so that the concierge wouldn't hear them come in, or perhaps so that she wouldn't be obliged to wake him by ringing the bell. Under the golden statue she embraced the doctor.

From that day on, Doctor Friedmann went to the house on Grand Transport Street every afternoon. The two hours that he spent there became the most important part of his day: more important than work, more important than attending his clinic, more important even than keeping in touch with his family. This is how the letter from his wife sent to his address at headquarters lay unread for four days. In it was the news that his elderly mother, already dangerously ill with coronary ischaemia, had worsened noticeably. The tersely-worded note from his colleague who was looking after the old lady left little room for hope, and anyone reading the letter would have set out immediately to be at her side. But on hearing the news Doctor Friedmann found himself facing a terrible dilemma.

'What shall I do with that poor child?' he asked himself, his hands pressed to his temples and his elbows on his knees. This was the thought in his mind that he was able to give voice to; the precarious state of his mother's health he felt only as a great emptiness in the cavities of his body. For two hours he stayed like this, immobilized. Then he got up, took the medicines he had smuggled out of the store cupboard and headed for Vera's house.

He felt that he was saying goodbye for ever to something that for the whole of his life had protected him from the inevitable knocks of fate and the facts of existence. From that minute on it would be a struggle to make it alive from one day to the next.

With every step he was coming closer to committing some offence he couldn't yet define precisely. But he was already aware of its awfulness and the corresponding demand for punishment. He was ashamed to be alive.

On the way to Grand Transport Street he stopped at the post office and sent two telegrams, one to his brother's address and one to his own, for his wife. Then he almost ran to the green house. Vera's mother opened the door the instant he arrived: she had obviously been waiting for him, peering out from behind the curtains.

'At last you've arrived,' said the woman, pressing her body close to his.

It was only after doing what they had done every afternoon for over two months with all the precision of a ritual that Friedmann had the courage to tell her he was leaving.

'I understand,' she sighed. She was in the habit of talking to herself in a whisper, so that now whenever she lowered her voice she seemed to be talking to herself. 'I understand perfectly.' There followed a long silence punctuated by the gentle breathing of the child.

'She's much better. She's getting up on her own. She's walking about. You just have to watch that she doesn't bump into the furniture. She is getting over her fits. I can't imagine life without her, it wouldn't make sense. Look, I have her medicine ready. If I should ever fall ill and no longer be capable of looking after her . . . You know I wash her twice a day, from head to feet. Sometimes I have to wash myself afterwards. Her dirt, her diarrhoea even gets into my hair, the poor thing.'

'Why are you telling me all this?' he said, trying to sound cutting.

'I don't know. But I believe she still has all the words in her head. Thoughts we can't even guess at. One day I'll tell you everything. But now go. You have to leave.'

Friedmann took the packet of medicines out of his pocket; he wore the look of a thief caught in the act of stealing. But not because of the stolen medicines. He was robbing himself of two people. He turned to go.

A ridiculous wail rose into the air of that wretched morning, almost like the boo-hoo-hoo of a mechanical doll. Vera's mother stood there in front of him in her nightdress, overwhelmed by despair.

'She's faking it,' thought Friedmann, 'there's not a tear in her eyes. And if she's not faking it, then so much the worse, for that means her emotions are ice-cold.'

'Boo-hoo-hoo,' came the cry from the mechanical doll, 'who will think of us?'

'What a difficult situation,' the doctor reflected, 'just my luck to have to make such a weighty choice. But I have to go. I can't leave my mother to die alone. I have to go.'

He thought it over at length; he even went as far as denying the priority of erotic over filial love. Finally he was able to wriggle out of the woman's embrace. Without so much as looking at Vera he turned and went. As he closed the door behind him he caught a glimpse of her little head raising itself from the pillow and he heard a quiet voice whisper his name.

Or was it just an illusion, a product of his guilty conscience?

'Choices, choices,' he repeated to himself as he walked along the streets, now full of people all of whom seemed to be celebrating something. 'Too many choices. I don't like it. There must be more to life than choices. It would be ridiculous otherwise. But it seems to be the rule.'

It was with a great sense of relief that, a couple of hours later, he was able to climb aboard the light aircraft that in various stages would take him back home. During the trip he jotted down some of his thoughts in a diary: 'Every evening, from the age of five, I have prayed that I would die together with all those I love and all those who love me. Now I have to watch my mother . . . But why should I complain? Perhaps it is better to live the torment of a life without laws than to die in a split second, with a split second of terrible pain. I suppose it must be like the pain of giving birth: one's whole life force gathers its strength in the belly, and then lungs and blood and muscles and bones all work together to expel the new individual. Except that in death one is expelling life itself from the body. A split second . . . it would be better.'

His mind would not leave this slow procession of thought for the length of the journey. He felt strangely guilty about living on if his mother died; he couldn't even imagine her dead. He didn't notice the sunset. The day's torture forced him to think and to reflect.

Arriving at his destination he found his mother unexpectedly well. 'You're the reason they let me stay,' she said openly with a smile. 'If you go, I'll go too, for ever.' She seemed a little shy, as if she felt her illness was somehow her fault, and she spoke to her eldest son with an affection that she'd never before thought appropriate.

His wife and son came to meet them at the hospital. 'What am I to say to them?' he asked himself, and then stayed silent, pretending to be overcome with emotion.

78

'Tomorrow I have to go away for about three days,' said his wife. 'A trip down south, to a conference organized by the association. I'm taking the boy with me. I'm sorry—it's not much of a way to celebrate your return.'

Friedmann felt hugely relieved. 'That's all right. I'll stay here in hospital to be near Mother,' he said. He was very fond of his wife and especially of his son. The boy felt an almost protective, even paternal, affection for his father. In response to the doctor's often eccentric monologues on medicine or on life he would reply: 'Yet another of your brilliant ideas!' And then, clapping his father on the back: 'Dad, Dad, you'll never change.' But you could hear the pleasure in his voice as he said it: it amused him that his father—or rather, his little boy—was the way he was.

Friedmann's wife on the other hand, beautiful, refined and at the same time sensitive, simply couldn't get used to her husband's way of looking at life. She couldn't get used to his curiosity—travelling round the world in search of some strain of bacillus whose identity he kept a secret—nor to his fervidly disorganized mind. 'One day it will all come to a halt,' was Friedmann's usual riposte. Now he wasn't so sure any more.

'There's a telegram here for you,' said his wife. 'I read it only because I didn't know when you'd be arriving. Is it something serious?'

The telegram was from Vera's mother, asking him to return immediately. The child was in danger, and only he knew enough about the case to save her.

He had that same feeling of emptiness that he had when he heard the news about his mother: a terrible, aching loss, unmitigated by any loss of consciousness. 'The child must not die,' he thought. 'The world would not be the same without her.'

His wife asked him what it was about.

'Oh, a unique case I came across quite by chance. Absolutely unique.'

'Dad, Dad,' his son interrupted, this time giving him a pat on the cheek. 'Not that again! We both know there's no such thing as by chance, at least not from one particular point of view. Why do you think I studied theology, Dad?'

His wife asked him not to pay any attention to the request. Doctors were exposed to far too much psychological pressure of that kind. He really couldn't afford to get involved. And anyway it was too late now, really much too late. The doctor promised not to give in. His wife and son left the next day and he went to his mother's house.

It had been years since they had slept under the same roof, and this, together with his resolve not to go back to Vera, made him feel young again. He spent the evening sitting beside his mother's bed looking at her kind face and listening to her soft voice. Together they spoke of happy memories, of the trials and certain successes of life and of his career.

But during the night the thought of Vera and her mother would not leave him. He couldn't sleep: the more he tried to picture all the earth's suffering multitudes and remind himself that death was a natural condition, the more those two feeble beings returned to his mind and to his senses.

Two days later another telegram arrived with a message even more desperate than the last. He talked it over with his mother.

'Yes, go, if that's what your conscience tells you to do,' she said. 'I won't hold you back. Don't worry about me. You have your work, your science, to think about.'

Friedmann's blood froze as he listened. His mother was so ill that he didn't feel able to discuss things completely candidly with her. Science had also taught him this: it's not always best to tell the truth. The whole business seemed much too complicated to explain.

'Why should I worry her with my emotional problems? She has already suffered enough. No, I'll spare her this final pain.'

On the fourth day he took her to dinner in a restaurant and they talked long and openly about the years of emigration, the suffering, the struggle for survival, the mishaps at school, the birth of his son. They recalled the funny events of his son's childhood with tears and laughter. They went to their beds in peace, as if the past had somehow served to plug the holes in the present.

At two in the morning the telephone rang. It was Vera's mother. 'I arrived three hours ago. I need to talk to you immediately.'

Before agreeing, Friedmann tried to weigh up everything that would happen and everything he needed to avoid and how to avoid anything which would compromise his relative equilibrium. Words, gestures, shouts, cries and every conceivable form of lie passed through his mind. He agreed.

Noiselessly he locked the door to his mother's bedroom. When Vera's mother arrived at the house, she found the gate, the outer door, the porch door and the door of the house all slightly ajar. Friedmann was relying on the intelligence of his persecutor. When he saw her in the doorway he took her arm and led her to the bedroom.

Before he had time to turn out the light she put her arms around his neck and whispered: 'Another minute without you and I'd have died.'

His mother having by now made as good a recovery as she was likely to, Doctor Friedmann was asked by the Ministry to return to Europe to continue his work there, since he was the only specialist they had in the field. In the meantime his wife and son had returned from the conference trip. On the morning of his departure, his son was particularly affectionate towards him and kissed him repeatedly on the cheeks as he was leaving. The doctor's mother was dressed up in her most elegant red dress with a pattern of black flowers; the hairdresser had come to the house at dawn to put her hair up.

'I'll be waiting for you, my sweet. I'll wait here and I won't go till you get back. You'll spend many more beautiful nights like these past few, while your mother sleeps on the other side of the door.'

His mother's declaration of complicity alarmed him deeply. 'My secret's out,' he thought. 'From now on anything could happen. But at least it shows that she really does know everything, and it means that there's someone I can be honest with.'

He decided to write to his mother every day and keep her up to date with everything that happened to him, the good and the bad. In that way his story would come out into the open; in a confused sort of way Doctor Friedmann was beginning to convince himself that his experiences were wholly exceptional, and that it was imperative they were documented.

They travelled separately, as they had arranged. Vera's mother departed one day before the famous scientist. On his arrival on 21 June, Friedmann reported to his superiors. The formalities completed, he was able, with the somewhat dubious consent of his general, to return to his previous lodgings in Acacia Avenue in the house of a widow who had lost her two sons in the war, and who treated him as if he were one of her sons brought back to life.

The first week passed without any news from Vera's mother. He resolved to put an end to their relationship and, if at all, to concern himself in the future with the child and only with her. He was aware, however, that circumstances cannot be changed quite that easily, neither for better nor for worse, and so he vowed that he would not descend voluntarily into that nest of vipers unless he received a specific request to visit the child.

He heard nothing from the woman. He continued collecting his statistics on diabetes. He wandered around the ruined neighbourhood, visited the sick for four hours every day, took notes, catalogued the cases worthy of most interest. And he wrote long letters to his mother in which he revealed the remotest thoughts of his waking hours as well as the labyrinths of his nocturnal visions. Every now and again his mother would reply with expressions—usually fairly conventional ones—of love and concern.

On his sixth day back in that strange and yet familiar country he was summoned to see the general.

'It has come to my attention that you are neglecting a case of the greatest interest for the treatment of neoplasia of the central nervous system. What sort of scientist are you? We know, among other things, that this case has been drawn to your attention on a number of occasions, to no effect. This is not any old mission: it's a scientific expedition, not a pleasure trip. I don't want to hear your excuses. Just get to work!'

An hour later the woman was in the arms of her lover.

'I have to go and meet my poor husband's stepmother,' she said, getting up and dressing hurriedly. 'She was so good to me, the poor thing, and to him. Now she's all alone in her bombed-out house. She has nobody in the world. Will you stay here with the child? I'll never ask you again, I swear it. I'll be back in an hour. Please, do me this favour. I don't like leaving Vera with the neighbours, like I did when I came to see you. I'm afraid they'll mistreat her. I have this terrible suspicion. And she, poor thing, can't speak, can't do anything. Will you forgive me for asking you this one favour?'

Friedmann was happy. For some time he had wanted to be alone with this creature who was such a mystery to him. But at the same time the man became aware of a vague sense of ill-boding which seemed to emanate from some deep and unknown part of his being, like the failure of some vital organ that was slowly spreading into all of his limbs.

'If I agree to do what this woman is asking I'll be stuck in this house for ever. I can feel it. But it was only to be with Vera that I've put up with all of this. I have given everything and everyone for this one opportunity. And now I am frightened and I'm trying to back off. It's grotesque.'

'It's no use,' she moaned through her tears. 'I can't let that dear old lady die of hunger. I'll take Vera to the neighbours. Or I'll take her with me, on my back.'

'Please don't. Leave her here. I'll wait till you get back. But hurry. Go to your mother-in-law.'

Vera's mother made herself up, dabbed herself with what was left of a bottle of perfume and left. As the door closed the doctor knew for certain that a part of his existence had finished for ever. He didn't know what would become of him from now on.

His heart beat loudly as he headed for Vera's room; he felt slightly ill, the way he used to at school when there was to be a test that day.

The child had been placed upright on a cushion just the other side of the door. As Friedmann entered he was harpooned by Vera's look. He struggled with himself for a moment, turned to go, then changed his mind. With one hand he wiped a drop of sweat from his brow, and with the other shielded his breast, as if to ward off a stabbing pain in his heart. Finally he calmed down enough to return the child's stare.

Her smooth, round face, her lips only slightly parted, her forehead, narrow, but high and even, her small perfect nose, all combined to the same effect, emphasizing her look of terrible mildness.

He sat down next to the child. The way he was acting, the clothes he was wearing, even the thoughts in his head seemed completely fake in the judgement of that purposeless stare. He felt a sense of shame, and wished that he too could be like that: exactly what he was, and nothing more.

'Little darling,' he said quietly. Something about the child filled him with a feeling of tenderness and respect such as he had never felt for anyone before.

A thread of saliva ran over the child's lower lip and dangled, extending little by little until it landed on her arm resting in her lap. Her legs were crossed and her hands held palms together in an attitude of absolute piety and gentleness.

'You have suffered so much, haven't you, little one?' the man asked, immediately aware of his own banality. But his impulses were now leading him from one ineptitude to another, almost as if he was trying to convince himself of his own worthlessness.

'My name is Abraham. Go on, try it. A-bra-ham.'

The child began to twist herself into unnatural poses which, if they didn't actually cause her pain, must certainly have been exhausting. Her head, almost completely hairless, followed the contortions of her body. Her eyes were almost closed, with just a tiny slit showing, enough to detect her constant stare, both present and absent at the same time.

'Come on, little one. Call your mummy, just like you did that morning on the landing. Call her, please. Ma-ma. Ma-ma.' The child stopped twisting and turned once again to face Doctor Friedmann. He was moved by the light of her expression.

'What can I do for you, little one? Do you want something? Is there something you'd like? Tell me what you want.' The child stared into a corner of the room.

'Who knows what thoughts are swarming in that little head of hers?' the doctor thought. 'Who can guess what she might have seen in that corner, or when? She's probably trying to evoke those memories now. Or maybe she really does see someone, someone we cannot see and will never be able to!'

'What was it you saw in that corner?'

Vera's features contorted into an expression that might be described as one of anger or of pain and remained fixed like that for what seemed like a long time.

'Is something wrong? What is it? Come on, tell me, please.'

The child didn't move. Another rivulet rolled off her lip, stretched in the air and dribbled on to her dress.

'I'm sure you know all the words to speak but don't want to use them. Why not? Go on, have a try. You're doing it to exasperate me, aren't you? You understand every word, but you're refusing to communicate with anyone because of the way they hurt you. Your mummy told me about your screaming fits, every night, for months and months after the first operation. You shouted at your father, your mother, your grandparents. And now you're getting your own back, right? Go on, say something. You're getting your revenge on the world for betraying you, aren't you?'

Speaking these words—which he later scrupulously noted down (or had they been altered by his memory?)— Doctor Friedmann gave way to the temptation to attribute ever widening significance to his interpretation of the facts.

The child became rigid. Her face turned red, then a darker colour, as if she were straining tremendously. Her eyes filled with tears and her neck swelled and swelled.

'She's trying to say something,' Friedmann thought, 'but she can't get it out. Perhaps she's forgotten how to speak. I must be patient.'

'My darling, my sweet, I love you, I love you more than anyone else alive. I love you without conditions. You're my heart, you're my angel, my soul, my everything. My little baby, my little baby.'

The man shuddered to hear himself speaking like this, so sincere and so false, to Vera. Tears filled his eyes, he wanted to throw himself to the ground, prostrate himself at the feet of that small, motionless figure. Suddenly he felt her little hand touch his cheek and the gesture, somewhat clumsy and uncontrolled, struck him as indescribably affectionate and sincere.

'My love, say something. Speak to me, my sweet, I beg you. Say Abraham, I implore you: Abraham.'

The child withdrew her hand and the expression of strain and tension disappeared, to be replaced by a look of disenchantment.

'Please, little one, I beg you with all my heart, in desperation, say something.'

Why did he want words? Why was he not content with the affection he had already been shown? Doctor Friedmann was unable to explain this to himself. It wasn't greed, nor was it poverty. It was something else.

His thoughts returned to the dream he'd had and he was filled with despair to see how obstinately reality refused to accord with it.

'I know you used to be able to read, write, play the piano. I know you used to dance beautifully. Where did it all go, tell me? And what are you now? What were you before you were born? What do you think of us, what do you see? How much life is left in you? Tell me about Rex, go on, tell me about your dog. Mummy told me everything. Rex, where are you? Bow, wow . . . Re-ex, Re-ex! Call Rex!'

Vera remained motionless and the expression on her lips reminded the doctor all of a sudden of the unfathomable misery of the hospital corridors: the excrement, the urine, the shame and the resignation of certain patients, and their tenacious hold on life, on illness and on death.

'Come on, little one, I won't torment you any more. Now I know you'll never speak again. But at least give me another little hug. Go on, give me another hug.'

The child did not move. She continued to look straight ahead, as if she were aware of her own smell, of her own filthiness, as if it disgusted her. But this pose made her appear even more graceful, arousing tenderness rather than pity.

'My love, my little darling, please give me another caress. I've been naughty to you. I won't do it again. Do you hear? Never again. Give me one more smile. Let me feel your gentle breath again, let me feel it deepen as you strain, or perhaps because you love me a little. Do like you did before.'

Vera shook her head, almost imperceptibly, as if to say: 'No, I don't want to.' Was it an illusion? Was it his state of excitement that made him think he saw the gesture? The man repeated his miserable request, he didn't hesitate to beg for Vera's affection. But the child didn't move.

'Why are you doing this? Are you trying to hurt me?'

With an effort that before would not have seemed possible, Vera began to pull herself upright; agonizingly slowly, pushing down on the arms of the chair, she managed to get to her feet. Her head and torso swayed wildly from side to side before she found her balance.

Then she began to walk towards her bed, one tiny step after another. The rays of the setting sun caught the outline of her figure and for a moment she appeared to be made of light. Vera's progress across the room was very slow. She pendulated from one leg to the other, looking as if she might fall at any minute to the right or to the left.

'Where are you going?' the doctor shouted. 'Stay here! You can't go hiding in your sleep! You're quite capable of sleeping all day and not saying a word to anyone. All you want is someone to dote on you, wait on you, feed and look after you, but you're not even prepared to give them a hug in return. I want to understand you! I want you! Do you hear? Do you hear?'

Vera reached her pitiful little bed with its satin-covered quilt the colour of gold. Gently she lowered herself down on to the edge of the bed. She was about to lay her head on the pillow when Friedmann took hold of her.

'No! You're not getting away that easily! I want to hear your voice! Can you cry?' The doctor took her by the shoulders and shook her hard. 'Let me hear your voice, now!'

The child's expression became even more vacant. A look of complete stupefaction flashed across her face, so breathtaking that for an instant the doctor's anger was stopped in its tracks. But the next moment his fury rose more violently.

'What is it? Are you surprised that I'm desperate? You don't think it might have been you who provoked me? You, you, you!' Friedmann began to rain slaps on her tender cheeks until they turned crimson. A muffled cry emerged from the child's throat.

'Louder! Louder! Let's hear what your voice sounds like!' The famous professor, the research scientist, was spotting the poor creature's face with blood. He wanted to hear her cry, louder and louder. He was aware of what he was doing, he knew how cowardly and how cruel he was being, and he knew that he was endangering Vera's life. The effort of holding himself back was making him sweat, but still he didn't stop until he saw blood mixed with saliva coming out of the child's mouth.

Vera was sobbing disconsolately, struggling to catch her breath.

'Darling, come here. Come here, and let's wash ourselves before mummy gets home. I won't do it again, I promise, I won't do it again. Come on little darling, come on my love.'

He tried to pull her towards the bathroom, but her body remained motionless. 'Come when I tell you!' the doctor shouted, tugging her roughly towards him.

And now the child's cries became louder and more desperate. 'Don't scream, they'll hear us!' he whispered, trying to cover her mouth with the palm of his hand. Finally he had to force his fist between her bloody lips.

He pulled a handkerchief from his pocket and wiped Vera's face, then sat her down on the sofa opposite him. When the child raised her eyes to meet his, Doctor Friedmann knew that judgement had been passed.

He took a sheet of paper and wrote a farewell note. Then he ran out of the apartment.

He arrived home bathed in sweat. Still out of breath, he stretched out on a couch and lay there pondering what he had discovered about himself that afternoon.

'I'll never feel at ease again. I'll never remove this stain of guilt, not even with my own blood. It's true: all I have to look forward to is a life of remorse, of atrocious suffering, infecting everyone around me with evil. Why did it all happen? How could I have acted the way I did? How could such cruelty have grown inside me? Or was it her, Vera? What is it within her that provokes such wickedness in an otherwise quiet soul? How could such an angelic looking creature evoke such injustice? It is her, it is her who's to blame!'

With this attempt to console himself, Friedmann dozed off, and as his conscience rushed headlong into sleep, it carried with it into the darkness the firm conviction that Vera was the cause of all his troubles.

At three in the morning he was woken by the telephone. 'I'm calling you now,' Vera's mother said, 'because in a few minutes' time I'll no longer be capable. So you want to leave me. You want to go. Well that's fine. I've taken care of everything: the child and I are fixed up for good. I'm so sleepy . . . I've taken some pills. I've taken so many . . . Too bad, we loved you. We loved you very much . . . '

Ten minutes later the doctor was once again in the dark belly of the Eighth District. He groped for the gate, and then found the door.

Vera's mother was stretched out on the quilt wearing a white nightdress embroidered with threads of yellow silk on the collar and bust. Her features looked relaxed in the light of the lamp on the dresser. An empty bottle of sleeping pills lay next to her hand, which was resting on the quilt as if she were about to play a chord on the piano. The whole posture of the body gave Friedmann the impression of artificiality. He sat down on the edge of the bed and listened to the mother's breathing. It was regular and quite strong: there was no question of coma. Then he thought he could see the woman peeping at him through closed eyelids; lying the way she was, he found the whole thing embarrassing. He went to examine the child. Switching on the lamp above her bed, he couldn't help sighing at the look of perfect calm on Vera's face: He felt as if he were committing an act of sacrilege just looking at her, and was surprised to find that he was still alive. Life implied the onerous obligation to act. It became even more onerous when every form of action appeared to the doctor indecent and ridiculous in the face of that dignified, absolute passivity.

He turned back to the child's mother. He had to slap her face repeatedly to bring her round. How often he had clasped that face, transfigured by passion, close to his chest! But what it was that moved her to such passion the doctor couldn't fathom. It certainly wasn't him; in his own opinion of himself, he was capable at most of evoking only pain or pity. Still she had chosen him to be the instrument of the emotions of her own body and soul. She had searched meticulously among the multitude of men for a compliant subject; and she had found him.

After two or three slaps on the cheek the woman came to. 'What are you doing here at this hour?' she asked the doctor who was appalled by the look of complete anguish on her face.

'What do you mean what am I doing?'

'Who let you into my house?'

'You did. I let myself in with the keys you gave me.'

'Keys? What keys?'

'You know well which keys I mean. Come on, get up, quickly, I'm taking you to hospital.'

'But I haven't done anything, I don't know what you're talking about . . .'

'You give me the keys then you don't know what I'm talking about. Don't be ridiculous.'

Minutes passed before she could be convinced that she had tried to kill herself by taking an overdose of sleeping pills. In her encounters with the doctor, Vera's mother was in the habit of trying to pass off as perfectly normal situations arising from her behaviour that were, to say the least, absurd. Perhaps it had been the protracted illness of her daughter, now accepted as a permanent condition and no longer thought of as something which might eventually come to an end, which had caused her to regard all the 'illnesses' of reality as quite normal occurrences. Vera's mother was completely at home in this eternity of sickness.

No sooner had she arrived at the hospital than she began to complain at how dirty and disorganized everything was. The nurses, veterans of the war and used to amputating arms and legs by the dozen, wouldn't look after her. She began to cry as she entrusted Vera to the doctor.

'Call the woman next door if you can't manage yourself, just don't let her die, I beg you. I didn't give her pills, I only took them myself.'

It occurred to the doctor that everything had been arranged so that he would be alone with Vera. As he returned once again to Grand Transport Street, he felt as if he were about to undergo the most decisive test of his existence and that the test was nothing more or less than the run to the finish. In fact he was afraid that his inadequacy with regard to Vera might have driven him to despair and to suicide. The child, on the other hand, symbolized for him an infinite duration: the spirit of life in her seemed indestructible. These thoughts both comforted and depressed him.

'She'll survive us all,' he thought, and then laughed bitterly to himself. 'We're all working to keep her alive, and dying in the process.'

When he arrived at Vera's house it was already dawn. He put out the light which he had left burning and turned again to stare at the child's pouting face. She looked as beautiful as ever in the bright rays of the moon. Friedmann resigned himself mentally to the situation. He had no idea how long this period of enforced togetherness would last, nor where to begin.

He fell asleep in a threadbare armchair which he had dragged into position alongside the child's bed. A short time later—or perhaps a long time later—he heard someone call out his name. He opened his eyes and saw Vera staring at him. She had called him! So she could speak! So it had all been a trick, an act, even her mother's attempted suicide.

Doctor Friedmann had slumped down a little into the armchair; now he adjusted his position, sitting up straight and looking solemnly ahead.

'Did you call me?' he asked the child, a little ironically. 'Here I am!' She didn't bat an eyelid. She just stared down at him, with the slightest hint of a smile in her eyes and in the corner of her mouth.

'If you can speak, why don't you tell me everything?'

The child remained silent, standing stiffly, her expression rigid on her face.

'Yesterday you reduced me to behaving like a wild animal,' he murmured. 'Today you won't succeed. You're trying to provoke me with your silence, but I won't fall for it.' But as he was saying these words, he was aware that he was in a state of near-delirium. That defenceless, motionless creature sitting opposite him wielded her power over him simply by existing, simply by being there. The paradox of her insistence on life made no sense to him, the scientist.

'Where did you learn to act like that? Standing there with one tiny hand on your cheek, your elbow raised, looking chaste and fearful, simpering and surprised. Where did you learn those gestures? Tell me! What are you trying to do? Seduce me?'

Vera's appearance moved the doctor almost to tears. 'Could anyone be wicked enough not to see in you a thing of beauty, not to want you for his own desires, to bruise your delicate flesh?' He was surprised by his own thought, but still he continued his peon. 'Men can be mad, perverse. But it's all part of life and the ways of nature. My little angel, my dear one, my beauty, my beauty . . .'

The doctor expected a little reward for his amorous words. But this time the child didn't move. Not a sound,

99

nor an embrace. But now from Vera's snow-white bed a new odour assailed the doctor's sense of smell, and he realized that from that moment on he would have to devote himself to the most humiliating tasks just to keep that tiny body clean, that as well as feeding her, moving her around and caressing her it would be his job to wipe up even the lowliest excrement of her delicate organism.

'It doesn't frighten me,' he murmured as he set about cleaning her up. 'I'll do it all; not out of sacrifice, but with great joy. This is my love for you.'

Some days passed—exactly how many, his diary doesn't reveal, perhaps because the same Doctor Friedmann had lost all sense of time passing. He stopped looking after himself, lost all interest in his own needs, and took to caring for Vera with punctilious precision. But beyond providing for all her daily needs he continued his attempts to penetrate her unconquerable silence and indifference. Every now and again, when the sun's rays shone red, he would take her on his knees and sing her songs, recite poetry, make animal noises, speak to her tenderly in different languages. There were times when he felt his childish rage returning and was on the point of losing control. But when that happened Friedmann would tense his lips and clench his fists, repeating to himself: 'I musn't go backwards. I must erase my mistakes, with other mistakes perhaps, but I have to change. I'm sure Vera's strength will return to her, and that her illness will not hold her back for ever. I have faith. The more she makes me despair, the more faith I have.'

Sometimes, having put Vera to bed when, either through laziness or sheer physiological impossibility, she was incapable of walking more than one or two steps, Friedmann would sit down, eat a piece of bread or an onion, and poke around in the drawers of the sumptuous chests in the apartment.

He found a pile of photographs, each with a precise caption on the reverse: 'Vera at one year old . . . at two . . . at five years old.' 'Vera the day before the operation.' 'Vera on the beach at . . . ' The names of some tiny places he had never heard of, which perhaps didn't even exist.

'Vera three weeks after the operation.' No visible difference. If anything she was more beautiful, much more beautiful now. But beautiful wasn't quite the right word.

He even found an old record with a label which read: 'Vera's voice.' He put it on the gramophone and listened. The flat voice of a spoiled child: 'Mummy loves daddy and daddy loves mummy. Vera loves mummy and daddy. The dog says bow-wow, the cat says miaow-miaow.' A woman's voice asks: 'How many fingers do you see?' and she answers: 'Seventy!' She laughs. At the bottom of an old suitcase he came across a number of exercise books. Each bore a white label with a blue border. 'Six years old.

Seven years old. Eight years old.'

Simple, rather banal phrases, repeated ad infinitum across the page between the thin grey lines. 'The sun shines. The rain falls. Birds fly. Snakes crawl. Plants grow.' The world she had created was obvious and monotonous and indicated a period where time had no meaning. But gradually, from one year to the next, the handwriting grew less distinct, the letters became bigger and bigger, until finally all that remained were gigantic scrawls.

'Vera says she wrote "today".' 'Vera says she has written "you".' 'Vera says she has written something but she is pointing at a blank space.'

One day Doctor Friedmann found an album containing photographs of the family's dead. The photographs, some of them rather mysterious looking, were stuck to sheets of black card and showed well-groomed, well-dressed men and women with radiant faces. Sacrificial victims, silent, composed, not a coarse gesture or a dissonant expression among them, conscious of the function of their own deaths. So many photographs. The doctor never would have believed she had such a large family. He remembered his own, still alive, and he dashed off a letter to his mother:

I'm getting used to this country, perhaps because I know that Father's father and even Father himself were born here. Once I would never have considered staying here, living in this part of the

102

world. Today the thought no longer shocks me. If you too wanted to return I think you'd be content here; 'happy' would be too gross a word—you know well how remote that possibility is for any of us.

Anyway, let me know what you think. My wife and son will of course say no. I'll wait for your answer before mentioning it to them. I cried a lot the other night thinking about all the love I would be leaving behind, but believe me, I absolutely have to stay here. Don't ask me to explain. Let's just say that I am compelled to by my desire to know, and for me that is more important than anything else.

By now the lie came so naturally to him that to say or write the truth—or a semblance of the truth—would have struck him as an unprecedented transgression.

Then one morning a series of loud knocks on the door brought the doctor back to the reality of the world outside. He didn't know whether he ought to open it or not. The house was by this stage in an intolerable state of disorder. An acrid smell of urine pervaded the air, and the triangular napkins he used to wipe the child lay in a soiled heap in the corner. Saucepans and plates were strewn about the table and across the wooden parquet floor.

'It doesn't matter; let them see my mess. I know I have to let them in, I sense that something good will come of it. My imprisonment is about to end.'

He opened the door. The general's adjutant was

waiting for him. 'I've been trying to reach you at your lodgings for days on end. I wanted to deliver this letter to you. The general wants to see you. I think he's a little angry. You disappeared completely. Do you know what they call that? Desertion.'

On the spur of the moment, the doctor couldn't think of anything better to say than to claim that he was only doing his duty as a scientist. But did this excuse stand up in the light of his duty as a soldier? The adjutant agreed with him but said that these things were decided 'very high up'.

It was only once the general's emissary had disappeared down the dark throat of the stairwell that Friedmann was able to recover a little of his calm and poise.

He opened the letter:

I have learned, from those who know you well, all about your infidelity and your ridiculous erotic intrigues. From this moment on you had better forget about me and about my son, whom you should no longer consider yours. We'll discuss the rest in court. You never loved anyone. Shame on you.
Your wife (but not for much longer)

Doctor Friedmann folded the letter, put it in the outside pocket of his uniform next to his heart, and turned to Vera. He ground some sleeping pills up in powdered milk, mixed it with a glass of water, and gave it to the child to drink.

After putting the child to bed, the doctor went out to face the general.

What a strange impression it made on him, coming out of the prison he had held on to so tenaciously! Compared to the rigours of Vera and the passions of her mother, so chaotic and yet so precise in her aims, the ruined city and the throngs of starving people in the streets seemed to him to be completely without purpose. The suffering on their faces, the piles of waste, the stench of filth, the crazed efforts at reconstruction were nothing compared to the child's mute dignity.

'This too is life, but real life is like Vera's,' he thought, and noted his thought down.

The Hotel Continental was full of women and soldiers in uniform. His fellow officers gave him a warm welcome —he was well-liked by everyone—and even the general greeted him in a friendly way, if a little stiffly.

'Sir, in contacting my wife you were interfering in our private affairs. I have not in any way acted against the interests of my country, or of the army, or of anyone else. By what right did you intervene? My conduct, as far as anyone knows, has always been rigorously within the boundaries of current standards of morality.'

'I know how much store you set by current standards of morality. Yes, and the boundaries are fairly flexible;

unfortunately there's a lot of hypocrisy around. But that doesn't change the fact that your conduct has been reprehensible, and I as your superior cannot tolerate that. Apart from anything else, that business with the child is highly suspect, I won't put it any more strongly than that, and if you can't give me an explanation right here and now, I will have no alternative but to . . . ' The general stopped.

'To?'

The general made a gesture of passive dejection. 'To punish you in an exemplary fashion,' he replied.

Punish him? Wasn't he already paying for his terrible, inexplicable violence towards Vera?

'Nevertheless you descended to the gutter in involving yourself in my private affairs. You wrote to my wife.'

'Your wife?' asked the general, raising his eyebrows. 'Your wife doesn't exist as far as I am concerned. I am not in the habit of writing to an abstraction.'

'Look what my wife wrote to me. Look.'

Doctor Friedmann pulled the letter out of the pocket of his uniform. The general glanced briefly at the crumpled sheet of paper, read a few lines, then, holding it between his index and his middle fingers, threw it down on the shining surface of his large table as if it were a playing card.

'Go away and take it up with someone on your level. You should be ashamed of yourself. From this day on as far as I'm concerned you don't exist. The machinery, not the person at the controls, will bring you to justice.'

The scientist left the building, not at all offended. The general's condemnation had been deserved, and he himself agreed with it. The only judgement that might have hurt him would come from the absence of Vera's look. 'And as for the anonymous letter, it must have been written by one of my fellow-officers. It's just what one would expect of an interfering colleague.'

He spent the morning making enquiries but was met with open laughter. By midday he was back at Vera's, none the wiser as to the identity of the secret informer.

He put the key in the lock with an increasing sense of discomfort: some old people were watching him from behind their windows as if he were a thief. Others were watching from the courtyard, their hands in the pockets of their worn-out dressing-gowns. What did those looks mean?

The key would not turn. The doctor tried and tried again, without success. 'What will become of the child if I can't get in? I'll have to break down the door. What awful luck! My life is going wrong at every turn. I'll never get it back on course.'

He put his shoulder to the door. The courtyard filled with spectators, silent and hostile. It was only to be expected of them.

Suddenly the door flew open of its own accord. In the

dark entrance he could just make out the slim figure of Vera's mother.

'I ran away from hospital. Come in, quickly, come in.'

The doctor had a sudden flash of inspiration: it made him desperately unhappy, yet at the same time he felt content, the way he felt after winning a game of chess.

'Was it you who wrote to my wife?' he asked nonchalantly.

Vera's mother closed the door with a smile. 'Don't bother asking me how I feel. Some welcome home!'

'I asked you a question and I'd like an answer,' the man shouted, perfectly conscious of the sad banality of the scene they were rehearsing.

'An answer? To what?'

'Look. Read this letter. Read what my wife has written to me. Who told her what I was doing, or what the two of you were doing to me?' He realized with horror that he was holding the child partly to blame. But perhaps she really was, and he was simply avoiding the . . .

'I see. You wanted to hide it all from your wife. You'd have preferred lying to this miserable truth. Shame on you. Well I didn't write anything to your wife.'

'Are you sure? You're not lying?'

'Quite sure. I'm not in the habit of telling lies. Still, if you insist on believing I did, then you can leave this instant. Vera and I don't need you.'

He hung his head. That evening, when he took Vera's

mother to bed, she showed him more passion than ever before.

The doctor fell into a sleep that was neither restful nor undisturbed: he felt a tiredness, a sort of deafness to the world which he had never felt before, and which he feared might turn out to be final and irreversible.

And yet in the depths of the night he got up, taking every care not to wake the woman, and tip-toed into Vera's room. He was naked, and the child appeared unflustered in the yellow glow of the nightlight. She looked at him: she looked at him and saw him, unmistakably, without the slightest reaction. He sat down and began to whisper quietly, telling her of himself, of his life, of all that he had had to leave behind him for ever, of past loves.

The tears fell on his bare knees and ran down his legs. Traces of expression flitted across Vera's face, disappearing as suddenly as they had appeared, until finally a faint sigh, a strangely prolonged and yet barely audible 'aah', issued from her lips: a sound without significance, or perhaps the sign of an intelligence that had understood everything and sympathized—for how could she not?—with all he had said.

These secret nighttime conversations continued for some time. During the day, Friedmann would get up only to eat, perhaps read a book, or make a few jottings in his notes. He moved all his belongings to the woman's house after informing the general of his decision. He wasn't ashamed of anything.

Vera's state of torpor, during which she was sometimes unable even to move her limbs or turn her head, ended suddenly one night. The evening before the child's mother had forgotten to make her take her sleeping pills. The doctor found her sitting on the edge of the bed, her arms waving, trying to enunciate some syllable, or possibly a word, that sounded like 'darling, darling'. As soon as she saw him she tried to stand up. Her nightdress had rolled down around her perfect, slender, tapering legs. The doctor ran to her fearing she was about to fall. He crouched down beside her and held her up. Then, quite unexpectedly, she put her little arms around his neck and began to kiss his cheeks repeatedly with inimitable tenderness.

'My love, my love! I knew this would happen. I knew there was more to you than mere silence. Come on, let's go to mummy. No man on earth has ever been happier than I am. My darling, my little treasure.' He began to cry, and the more emotional he became, the more the child seemed to understand and to want to help set him free from the unhappiness inside him.

Many happy weeks went by. The scientist didn't stop to wonder what unforeseen coincidence had caused the neuron circuits in that enormous mass of cells crammed into Vera's little head to start working again. Now she would speak his name every other minute, with such charm that she was able to transform the distressing appeal into a game. And her mother too found the child showing unusual confidence and affection towards her: Vera would stroke her face, press her little hands into hers, nuzzle her mother's forehead with her own. She had even recovered the strength in her legs, and on sunny afternoons all three would go for walks through the narrow streets of the neighbourhood, once again teeming with life after the rumble and the silence of the war. Vera walked in the middle and the doctor and her mother each held a hand. It seemed that she had grown a little and now looked nine or ten years old.

But the two people who knew her secret were a little anxious for her.

'Can it be that she has started growing again?' her mother asked, and the doctor replied with some elusive, meaningless and quite unintelligible scientific explanation.

But knowledge was of no use to him any more. 'I am overcome with happiness: I would never have believed that she could harbour so much affection, or that life could offer moments like this, that such joy was possible on earth.'

It had been worth sacrificing his other affections and duties. Now everything had a meaning for him. 'My wife and my son don't need me. And as for my mother . . . I'll see her again soon, I'll bring her here to live with me.'

The young body of Vera's mother no longer radiated agonizing distress in their lovemaking; now he found her presence reassuring. Doctor Friedmann had settled for once and for all the old doubt that nagged inside him about the goodness of man's existence on earth.

One Sunday afternoon they went into the pastry shop on Wednesday Street. They wanted to buy Vera some chestnut purée. As she saw the jar filled with threads of purée, her face lit up in happiness and gratitude, quickly replaced by the sly look of someone congratulating herself on having got exactly what she wanted by sheer cunning. The very next moment, without the slightest warning, Vera collapsed on the stone floor of the shop. The thud of her tiny head as it hit the floor was the most terrible sound Friedmann had ever heard. He was shaken to the bones, as if the sound heralded death itself. Not the child's death, or his own: the death of everything.

'My God,' cried Vera's mother in a thin voice that was almost a squeak. She began to cry over her daughter's motionless body. When Friedmann reopened his eyes the first thing he saw was Vera's bewildered look, her stare begging him to tell her what had happened.

'Why did this have to happen? Why does evil always have to visit this little creature? Why does it get mixed up with love and grace?'

Faced with the absurdity of this hysterical line of questioning, the doctor took refuge in logic and science.

He concluded that the scars of the operation, the prolonged use of drugs had probably caused permanent damage to Vera's cerebral tissue. Stopping the administration of the drugs, however, had probably led to a short-lived state of equilibrium which was neither controllable nor repeatable.

Throughout the next night the child's mother tried with great skill and some malice all her usual approaches, in a vain attempt to produce some reaction. In the end she fell asleep in a sulk, almost offended.

Friedmann got up and went to Vera. He stared at her by the light of the bedside lamp and stroked her head. He knew then that the feeling of complete happiness of the past weeks would never be his again. He told the child of his feelings, without pretending to hold a conversation, but in the sure conviction that she understood his every word, and much more than his words.

But Vera had once again shut herself away, absent and indifferent to him and to the world.

'Very well, I'll simply observe progress, and I won't make any more demands of you or of myself.' But moments later he wailed: 'Where have you gone to, and why?'

He loved her, without nourishing any hope, without any expectations; he was ready to confront the worst. He fell asleep in a chair beside the little white bed and when, the next morning, Vera's mother woke him, he realized he could no longer stand being near her.

They stopped going out together. The weather turned ugly. Another fit might cost Vera the loss of a tooth, or a fractured arm. Her perfect body was in danger, and with it Doctor Friedmann's life.

One night, rather than try again to communicate with Vera, he decided to continue another investigation. His suspicions on the subject of the anonymous letter to his wife had never been fully allayed and now he wanted to arrive at the truth. Why was the letter so important to him? It was obvious that he was looking for someone to blame for his fate.

Around five in the morning he began to caress Vera's mother's body tenderly. He started at her back, and when he felt her move, murmured sweetly: 'Was it you who wrote to my wife?'

The woman smiled in her sleep, stretched her limbs and mumbled a clear 'yes.'

His fury was immediate. He took her by the shoulders and began to shake her. 'Say that again, that you wrote to my wife. Say it again!' Her eyes flew wide open and she winced with the pain, but the doctor was not moved to stop.

'You wretch, it was you who took me away from everything good and sane in my life. Why? Why did you do it?' He repeated his ludicrous question five or six times, and when there was no response, he began to punch her

114

in the face. 'You evil monster, you!'

Any attempt the woman might have made to cry for help was masked by her gasps for air. She panted and flailed about desperately in an effort to ward off the scientist's blows, which were becoming more ferocious by the second. 'Are you trying to destroy all that's good in me? Are you trying to drag me down into your cess, into your nothing, you bitch?'

The man no longer knew what he was doing: he was punching wildly at Vera's mother in an attempt, however blind, to lay all his own guilt and failure on to her.

'Are you mad? You'll kill me! Are you trying to kill me?' The woman's voice was flat, nasal, rather faint. Its sound infuriated him all the more. Yes, it would be better if she didn't exist. But now, even if he were to kill her, he could not wipe out her existence, merely shelve it.

'You're killing me!' wheezed the woman, ceasing for a moment to defend herself. In that instant he became aware of what he was doing. He ran to the bathroom, locked himself in, started to wash the blood from his hands, and then with a shout smashed his head against his image in the mirror on the bathroom wall.

Dear Mother,
I'm writing to you again from here. Will you listen to me, just this one more time? I need you like I did

when I was a child. I need your love, I need you to encourage me to get on with my studies, to get on with life! This time I'm not asking, I'm begging you to come and see me in this country where my fate is working itself out. I could leave quite soon, indeed I ought to, as you know; the international agreements stipulate that our unit should leave the country now and hand over to other foreign forces. But whatever happens I can't not stay here. Let's say that I have chanced upon the most interesting case of my career; but let's say also that I have become completely embroiled, body and soul, in a relationship which I am unable to bring to an end. We two have never been completely sincere with one another, but now I feel we must. Please agree to come and start a new life here with me. We're now the only members left alive of our original family. Our roots are here, even if they're hard to see these days. I will live for you as long as you come and rescue me, haul me out of the damnation from which I can't seem to save myself. You know it's useless to expect anything of Lilian and Michael: for them I'm already dead. Answer me, please, with haste.

Appealing to you for help,

Your son.

P.S. If you don't understand my situation, if I sound crazy, remember that I didn't ask to be born. If nothing else, then at least take your share of the responsibility for having cast me, from your belly, into the world.

His mother, seventy-five years old and afflicted with serious illnesses and disabilities, replied in a letter written in lines which became more and more tightly packed together as they neared the bottom of the page. It was full of justifications, digressions, evocations of events both happy and sorrowful, of characters and sayings from the past. In short, it was a listless refusal of his request. The letter held out no prospect for the future beyond a patient and resigned wait for death to arrive.

The carpet has unrolled before our feet and we are reaching its end. Only one more step to go. Let us take it at the appointed time and in peace. We can't turn back because there is nothing behind us: as we tread the carpet, it is consumed. So, dear son, you too should be content with your lot, and if you really wish me well, then come here to live with me until the end of my days, or until the end of yours. No one knows precisely when his hour will arrive: the young sometimes go before the old, the healthy before the sick. It is useless to protest. I'll wait for you, then. But if your interests, science, your career, your feelings force you to stay, don't have any regrets on my account, stay, and don't worry about me. I'll take the last step alone.

Kisses and all my love, which will never change,

Your mother.

As Doctor Friedmann read and re-read the letter, far-away images of a remote childhood paraded before his eyes and all around him in the void. This is how he arranged the figures of his imagination. He sensed the presence of someone else inside him, a smaller copy of himself, a little boy. The boy was running quickly through the streets, forcing a way through the crowds, singing a canticle. Then suddenly his double receded, contracted around his worn-out body and disappeared inside him

'There, I've settled my scores with the past,' he said to himself. 'Now I can devote myself to the agony of the present.' It didn't occur to him to exert his own will, to take steps to change his condition. He thought of himself as an inert object confronting the relentless advance of events that would overwhelm him, trample him underfoot, and annihilate him.

'How on earth did I get myself into this state? It must be due to nervous exhaustion, a psychosis perhaps. Or maybe there really is something poisonous at work to undermine all of us, and everything else is an illusion? This is a fine trap we're in.'

He looked at Vera's face, her precise features, her unchanging expression, the barely perceptible flicker in her eyes, a sly, slanted look. 'It is her I'll live with from this day on. But I'll never understand her. It's useless. Before her all I can do is remain inert. We can compete to see who is the most inert.'

He began to stay in bed, in his pyjamas, until late in the morning, by which time Vera's mother had long since returned from the market and begun to cook and clean.

'Good morning darling,' she would say to him when she saw him appear in the kitchen. 'Do you still love me a little?' This phrase sounded like some horrible joke to him. It made his blood pressure rise instantly. His head would begin to throb with discomfort. The woman's question sought to burden him with a responsibility he had never asked for, in the same way as he had never asked to be born.

'Not only do they want us to live, although after a bit there's little good in life: they want love as well, they want us to love.' The thought scandalized him.

'Yes, I love you,' was his usual reply, before going back to bed until lunchtime.

'There's always the possibility that life itself will finish me off. What's that pain in my chest? Maybe I'm having a heart-attack! My fingers are going numb. I've a shooting pain in my arm. This may be it. I don't have the will to resist. Why should I?'

Meanwhile Vera's mother looked after all his needs: he couldn't have found anyone more useful, more loving or more dedicated to him. And Vera sat on her little sofa—

she had now started to walk again, with difficulty—and stared ahead, stared into eyes of Doctor Friedmann and her mother. 'There's something wrong, isn't there?' said her look. Every now and again her eyes would moisten, her stare would become unbearably intense, she was transported by who knows what visions: these were her moments of crisis. It was as if she had been carried off to another world, to the origins of being. There was no lying or pretence about her; her condition unmasked everything and everybody.

Day and night, in his thoughts and in his feelings, Friedmann scrutinized his own entrails. He was waiting for a sign which would announce the end. In reality he would not admit the fallibility of his own body: he wanted to die of no cause, not weakened by illness.

One morning, after the woman had gone out on her usual trip to do the shopping, he heard a knock at the door. The doctor didn't reply.

'Friedmann, open up! We have to talk!' It was the general's voice. He had come all the way here for him!

The doctor rushed to open the door. A moment later the gaunt figure of the general stood before him.

'Yes, I have come in person,' he said. 'I must speak with you.'

'With me? You?'

'Yes, as a friend. We were both born in this country. We grew up here and in America. Your behaviour has

120

been most irregular and . . . but just look at the way you're dressed.'

'Do you mean this dressing-gown? It belonged to the child's father. He is dead. Now I'm wearing it. Until I die too.'

'What child? What are you talking about?'

'I'm sure you've found out all about my situation, so please speak frankly.'

'Are you asking me to dispense with the pretences, is that what you mean? Social conventions, politeness, our whole existence, all meaningless next to Vera, is that what you're trying to say?'

'Yes, but there's one more thing I have to add,' Friedmann interrupted. 'Everything is meaningless, except blame. That solidifies as the rest evaporates,' he said whispering each syllable distinctly. 'I am twice guilty.'

'Fine, fine, but remember that a man must never condemn himself. He must be judged by others, for he cannot rise above his own person. Come away from here. In America we'll think it all over.'

'America . . . America. No, I can't. And anyway I don't need to think anything over.'

'You're right, why should you? When you're at the centre of an event you don't believe in the existence of other events, ones that were there before and ones that will be there after. It all gets submerged in the moment, blinded by the moment. Look at Vera: for her, the moment does not exist. In short: our mission is finished here. We're going home. Don't be a stubborn fool. Come with us!'

'No,' said Friedmann, with such firmness that the general took several steps backwards, as if the words had struck one of his legs.

'I'm staying here for ever. There's nothing else I want to do. I want to stay here.'

'You may not want to do anything else, but you do have obligations. And you can't simply duck them.'

'Obligations?' Friedmann demanded, motionless. 'What obligations? The obligation to live?'

'Yes, and to help others to live.'

'No, I can't think that far. Help who to live?'

The general hesitated for a moment. 'Your mother. Your son. Your wife.'

'I see. What came before, what came after, what came during. No. Prosecute me if you like, hand me over to the authorities, but I won't do it. That's not my job. I have still a lot to do today. Would you be kind enough to leave me to my tasks?'

'You have nothing to do, that I know. Don't you realize what it smells like in here? Open the windows.'

'Thanks all the same. It suits me fine.'

'So, you've decided you want to die?'

'What do you know of life and death? Go away.'

The general signalled to the two military policemen to take Friedmann away by force.

'Just one more day, I beg you,' the doctor pleaded, with unexpected humility. 'Just give me one more day. You don't know what scientific curiosity means. By tomorrow I may have discovered what I've been searching for all these months. This is a unique case, there isn't another one like it anywhere in the world. To have survived so long . . . I have to take one last set of samples, we can have the analysis done on the plane. Just one more day, please. For the sake of our childhood friendship . . . '

'Let him go!' the general said, and he left without a word, without even looking at him.

Going over what had happened in his mind, Friedmann knew that the general had not been the slightest bit taken in by his inventions and had only let him be to shame him all the more. 'But I won't let him, I swear I won't let him. He doesn't know how desperate my love can be. It's a pity I'll never see Vera's eyes and little face again. I'd like to know what she'd think if she were to see me in this state.'

What form should he choose for his own death? Yielding to his nightmares he pictured the nine hundred and seventy-six ways of dying he'd read about in some book. He began to sweat and felt faint. Now all he was waiting for was the moment of true decision. He went to Vera's room. He heard the gentle breathing of a creature who was full of grace and innocence, but terrible in condemnation. 'No, I will not be moved. I'll go my own way.'

And yet some moments passed before he had the courage to look into that face, to see her little hand resting on her cheek in her characteristic expression somewhere between chastity and pain, her arm bent, her elbow in the air. 'I'll go my own way,' he said loudly and turned to go out of the room. As he reached the door he heard her whisper his name.

'She called my name again! This time I won't react.' But the syllables of his name were hurled in his direction for a second time, this time louder than before. He turned around. 'Don't do that. Do you understand? Don't do that.'

The face of the child—but she was seventeen years old!—was relaxed and calm. Her eyes under her lids were indifferent, but alive. 'Why are you calling me? Tell me, why are you calling me? Would you call to anybody or do you just do it with me? Tell me!' He ran to the bed, took the child by the shoulders and shook her, shouting 'What do you want from me? Are you trying to hurt me again? I won't allow you to. No! And I won't let you see me dead. You'll come with me, wherever I go, you're coming too. I know nothing about you, but now it no longer matters.'

He ran into the kitchen and gathered all the bottles of

pills and a jug of water. 'We'll drink it together, it's nice, you'll see, it's nice.' He emptied the contents of five bottles, all that was left in the house, into a mortar and began to grind them up. The mortar rang like a bell under the blows of the pestle. He emptied the powder into a glass of water and turned to Vera.

'Yes, I've brought you some nice lemonade. Now we'll drink it together.' The contents of one bottle would have been enough to kill them both. Friedmann put the glass down and took Vera on to his lap. He began to sing an old lullaby, crying as he sang. He was deeply moved and felt that he was engaged in an act of great solemnity; it was a feeling he had felt as a child when, on certain holy days, he would put on his blue suit and his white shirt.

But before and after had vanished from his head. All that existed now was Vera's face and his own ego, a formless entity, and one that space and time would soon be rid of.

He raised the glass.

'Drink, my love. Whatever, whoever might be inside you no longer matters. It will remain our secret, your secret, for ever.'

Vera was staring at him, more intensely than usual. Her perfect lips, her nose, her clear brow, her cheeks, now a little pale, and unrelentingly soft, all these were beyond Friedmann's sense of awareness. Caressing the nape of her neck with one hand, he brought the glass to her lips with the other.

'My dear, sweet, innocent little creature . . . ' Slowly and carefully he poured half the contents of the glass into the red cavity of her mouth. Vera swallowed. 'It's over,' he thought with relief. He brought the glass to his own lips. And now all his feelings arose from the bottom of his heart like a swarm of dreadful insects, a terrible chord that came from within him, and yet also surrounded him. He was drowning in an ocean, but he was the ocean: an ocean of bitterness without end and without hope. 'Where to now?' he had time to wonder. 'Into nothing? Into nothing at all, or is there someone else still watching over me? An answer, before I cease to exist. An answer, I beg you!' He drank the first draught.

That instant Vera gave out an awful sound, a deep, tuneless, coughing, belching sound. The liquid she had swallowed came rising out of her stomach and spewed over Doctor Friedmann's face. She stared at him with moist eyes, her expression that of someone who has just done something unforgivable. She blinked, perplexed, but freed.

'So I have to go through with it alone! You've killed me. You've tricked me. The two of you will live and I will die. No matter. I won't turn back. I've reached the end of the carpet and there's nothing behind me, except for the two of you, except for the two of us.'

He raised the glass again but it flew out of his hand,

smashing into fragments on the worm-eaten wooden floor of the old house.

Vera's mother stood behind him. She had arrived just in time. 'But why, my love? Why did you want to leave me?'

She took his head and pressed it to her breast. But Friedmann pushed her away, threw the dressing-gown around his shoulders, flung open the door of the house and walked out into the blinding sunlight.

He wandered through the Eighth District.

His admission to the neurological ward of St John's Hospital, his stay in the mental asylum on Lime Tree Mount, his return to America and his participation in the Korean War are not relevant to this story. Nor are the circumstances of his disappearance in that far away corner of Asia something we can go into here.

Doctor Friedmann's notes and his diary were delivered to his legitimate wife ten years later, and her agreement to having them examined has made this reconstruction possible.

It is said that Vera and her mother moved to the Stone Quarry district. There is no documentary evidence that they ever stayed there.

When a man is ill, they decide on his life and death in the Fourth Palace. No man should pass judgement on himself, lest someone hear it and try to carry out sentence. The world exists through secrets. In the dream that Friedmann had shortly after getting to know Vera, they talked together for a long while, but when he awoke, the words were gone. There is no evidence that they ever came back to the illustrious, if unlucky, man of science.

A. Friedmann, *US Army Magazine*, Connecticut, 1945, pp. 164–166

BAHDY'S DISEASE

Speaking of Bahdy's Disease, these days increasingly widespread throughout the world, brings to mind a case I observed over the course of twenty years or so. I can still see the three patients in my mind's eye. Three patients—but only one disease. I always picture the three brothers together, but in fact I never saw them all at once. They came to me—why to me anyway?—at different times, with years between each visit. After the initial consultations, the diagnoses, the prescribed therapies, I was unable to follow the course of their illnesses any further: the men simply refused to undergo treatment. It was only from what the second brother told me that I found out what had happened to the first, just as the third was able to shed light on the fate of the second. What became of the last brother I never did find out.

It's all coming back to me now: I'm sitting in my old surgery in Karfenstein Street. I can almost taste the fresh

131

raspberry drink made for me by old Esther, my nurse at the time.

The May sun was streaming through the window and the syncopated footfalls of a cripple echoed in the silent afternoon. Someone opened the door to my surgery and then closed it again with extreme delicacy so that I hardly noticed the noise of the handle and the click of the catch. I looked up from the prescription I was writing and saw in front of me a man who seemed suffused with a radiant glow. He would have been about thirty as I remember him: slim and broad shouldered, his thick brown hair combed back from his brow, he stood upright in front of me wearing a calm, somewhat ironic expression. On his left arm he carried a light raincoat. He smiled at me with shy embarrassment, but without a trace of fear or cowardice. His chief concern seemed to be to preserve a sense of decency, to appear neither pathetic nor sentimental. He introduced himself, then took another step before stopping again. I indicated to him to sit down, which seemed the pragmatic thing to do, and noticed as I did—I remember this so well—that I felt slightly ashamed, the way no doctor ever should, that I was about to intrude on the privacy of this patient's body.

On examining him, I could feel a lump about the size of a walnut on the distal part of his right thigh. It could have been a cyst or a tumour, or perhaps the consequence of a muscle trauma caused by a sudden movement, or by

132

a blow from, or a collision with, a blunt object. Or it could have been a lipoma, a deposit of fat. I advised him to make an appointment to see a surgeon, gave him the address of a clinic where the friend with whom I played tennis worked, and asked him to come back after the operation with the results of the biopsy.

The summer passed. I spent a long, relaxing holiday on the lakeside. My wife and my children, young at the time, treated me to day after day of quiet charm.

One afternoon in September, before my clientele of teenagers and little old ladies had gathered in the darkened waiting-room to collect their pills against pimples and hypertension, Esther announced the return of my strange patient. Moments later the man with the raincoat on his arm appeared in my doorway and the surgery was filled with the solemn air of a holy day. I was never able to explain to myself where this atmosphere came from, nor indeed why he always carried the raincoat. At first I thought it was a somewhat aristocratic affectation, or perhaps a prop for the man's lack of self-confidence, or maybe even a nod at the English style. Only some months later, thinking of him quite by chance by who knows what chain of associations, did it occur to me that this article of clothing might actually allude to a permanent state of departure, even of flight. What response was he looking for in displaying this sign? Understanding? Pity? Or the *coup de grâce*?

I opened the sealed envelope and rapidly scanned the results of the biopsy and the many tests and analyses. His was a very rare case of a tumour, not of itself unfavourable, which grows in the connective tissue. Today it even has a name, histiocytoma. Our knowledge of it in those days, however, was scanty, and very confused. Some sources talked of pulmonary metastasis in thirty per cent of cases, others disputed these statistics. All were agreed however in tracing the tumour's origins right back to the embryo. In other words, the man's destiny had been stamped in his tissues since birth. As is the case with many of us. Whether the already disordered cell would, in the body of the adult, migrate to an arm, or to the chest, or swell the right foot seemed to be down to the luck of the draw, if one could admit to the existence of such a thing in our universe. But the significance of the cancer, which tomorrow we may call by another name, and which in the not too distant future will most likely have disappeared forever, was not something that the young man could find words for. For him, in that context, it was unsayable.

I was very unsure about how to break the news to him. I think perhaps I underestimated his intelligence and his education. But in the end it was he who came to my aid— how often patients come to the aid of their doctors!— excusing himself for having put me in a difficult position.

'I've done a little reading on the significance of the

diagnosis,' he said with a smile, 'and I can see that there's nothing particularly unusual about my case. In fact, I wasn't sure whether I should even come back—after all, why should I bother you? But I thought it might seem rude if I ignored the usual formalities. You told me to come back with the results of the analysis, so here I am. I know you can't do anything to save me. But you have to carry out your check-ups, make your deductions, prescribe and give advice all the same, you poor man. Just don't ask me to go into hospital. It wouldn't help—I'd feel you'd written me off.'

I wanted to comfort him, to lie to him, to try and get him to believe in miracles, to talk of possible cures. But after only a few sentences he interrupted me most politely.

'Thank you, Doctor,' he said with good-humoured irony, 'you've given me a new lease of life.' His voice was deep and reassuring, his face gentle but disillusioned. 'Well, I suppose that's about it. I settle up with the nurse outside, do I?' The heavy tread of his footsteps soon disappeared down the length of the corridor. I didn't even hear the outside door close, as if he had faded through the wall, just as histiocytes pass through the capillary walls in diapedesis.

I felt a wave of gratitude towards my patient for having spared me the awkward lies and the agonizing scenes. And then I forgot him, as I had forgotten so many others before him. Complete indifference is the only sort of humanity vouchsafed to those who care for their fellow men. Any sort of involvement—physical or emotional—would make helping impossible.

The years which followed saw my earnings increase and my career advance. I was invited to teach pathological anatomy at the University of M, a great honour in such a small city. But I didn't give up my surgery in the capital. I preferred to travel up and down three times a week than to content myself with making a reputation in a dull and unprofitable small-town practice.

It was May again—just a few days before it had snowed unexpectedly—when I made the acquaintance of the second brother. There would have been about three years difference in their ages, five at most. The second brother bore a striking resemblance to the first, both in appearance and in manner, even down to his dress. And yet seeing him didn't bring the other case to mind; as far as I was concerned it had been resolved—if not triumphantly—and wiped without a trace from my memory. Not even when he told me his name did I make the connection. In those days my memory was full of good things.

Only that, on looking up, I was struck by a look of radiance—that word again—on the man's face. He must have been about forty, well-dressed and elegant, a lawyer, I'd have guessed. He was standing in front of me, a smile on his lips and a look of humility in his eyes. He described in simple terms the pain he'd had for some months in his right calf every time he walked up a slope or climbed three or four stairs.

'The lift in our old apartment block breaks down fairly often. The apartments themselves are nice and spacious, but the old plumbing and antiquated electrics are a bit of a nuisance.'

It was as if he was attributing the cause of his own illness to entirely extraneous circumstances. But I wasn't having any of it. Patients, when they're describing their symptoms, often try and confuse doctors, hoping that fooling us into making a less serious diagnosis will actually change the nature of their illness, perhaps moving it from one organ to another. I had him undress and examined his leg.

And while I was doing it—I'm only realizing it now—I felt exactly the same sense of shame as I had done a few years before. Still I didn't make the connection.

Stretched out on the rubber sheet, the second brother stared at me throughout the examination. From my point of view it was all a bit of a sham—the examination, the diagnosis, everything. I had already made up my mind what the trouble was.

And then all of a sudden he said: 'The reason I came to you, Professor, was because you looked after my brother so well.'

'Is that right?'

'Yes, he told me so much about you. "An extraordinary doctor", he called you.'

'I'm glad I was able to cure your brother,' I said, without the faintest idea who he was talking about.

'Cure him? No, unfortunately you weren't able to cure him. You didn't even try. But he still spoke very highly of you.'

'That's strange,' I said irritably, my pride a little wounded, 'I don't remember that. I remember your brother well, of course, but I had assumed . . . What was it he had? Remind me, if you would. I have so many patients in my care . . . '

He told me all about his brother's case, and how he had died only a few months before. 'And now it's my turn. I think I have the same illness. The symptoms are very similar, identical even. If you find it difficult, if you'd rather not see me turn white, then just write it all down on a prescription form and I'll read it at home.'

And at that precise moment the memory of my strange patient of a few years before came flooding back. I felt a pang of regret that he had died. I spoke comfortingly to his brother, reassuring him that his illness was quite different to the other, and advised him to have further clinical investigations. But as I said, my prognosis was already made, and according to it the outlook was not good. The right superficial femoral artery was partially obscured and in a few years it would lead to paralysis if a coronary or something else didn't finish him off first. The pipework was becoming blocked up, just like in his old apartment.

He too returned to the surgery a few months later. He brought with him folders full of X-rays and analyses, charts and electrocardiograms, and letters with their sentence written in Latin, clear and irrevocable.

Much of an individual's destiny has already been decided centuries before he comes into being—in this respect the machinery of the human body doesn't leave us much room for manoeuvre. The judgements handed down by science are more severe than the sentence of a court; in the end, there's not much that any one of us can do or say that's really relevant in the grand scheme of things. History itself is but a tiny scrap of that enormous fabric of death from which life on our planet has sprung.

The second brother handed me the pile of papers and limped off, his raincoat on his arm.

That year I closed my surgery on Karfenstein Street. Old Esther had died of viral hepatitis and with her a family tradition disappeared. What reason was there to stay in that street when I could move to an elegant part of the city, to Rose Hill or Liberty Mountain? The prospect of the change seemed enormous to me, like moving from one universe, or world or century to another. What would await me in those *fin de siècle* suburbs? I threw out the old leather armchairs that had belonged to my father—once the best diagnostician in the city—and fitted out my new surgery with fashionable furniture and the most up-to-date equipment. The grace of my new nurse Martha, a shapely blonde whose young body was as fragrant as the plains she came from, lent an idyllic atmosphere to the hours I spent at work. My wife for her part provided me with the cosy and undemanding love of the perfect conjugal relationship. Those were the happiest years of my life.

I obtained the chair in comparative anatomy in the science faculty of the capital's university. I was assiduous in keeping up with developments in my field; I neither chased breathlessly after every novelty, nor resigned myself to a life of leisure.

One afternoon last year, when the streets were already covered in muddy snow and I was making plans to take a nice winter holiday, Martha took a strange call for me. She entered my office quite out of breath.

'Excuse me, Professor, but there's a patient on the line who insists on speaking to you at all costs. He won't listen to reason.'

'Just put the phone down on him and leave it at that,' I said with a smile.

'I've done that twice already,' she said 'but this gentleman won't give up. He phoned back straight away, both times. He's very upset.'

'Very well, put him through to me, but don't let it

happen again. Can't you see I'm with a patient?'

In fact there was a girl stretched out quite naked on the examination couch, her shining body demanding my absolute attention.

I went to the telephone. 'Professor, help me, please. You're my only hope. I've been confined to bed for the last three years. Save me, I beg you. You're the only one who can help me.' Without asking what the matter was I advised him to call an ambulance and have himself taken to hospital.

'No, please don't turn me away. You looked after my two brothers, you were so good to them, now you're almost one of the family. Don't abandon me, I implore you.'

The man—who from his voice must have been fifty, possibly sixty—was pleading in utter desperation.

'But what is wrong with you, what are your symptoms?' I asked him as calmly as I could. 'I might not even be the specialist you need.'

'Please come, I beg you,' he insisted in heart-rending tones.

What could I do? My sense of humanity, my studies in geriatrics, and my image of myself as a doer of good deeds, even as a sort of miracle-worker, struggled against decades of ingrained professionalism which called for absolute resistance to emotional blackmail. On the other hand, the little old men and little old women who used to visit me at my old surgery considered me a sort of demigod, only because I never refused them their weekly prescription of diuretics and laxatives.

I hesitated for a moment, and the man, bursting into tears of despair, knew it.

'Thank you, thank you, Professor. May God bless you. Come, come today or I'll die.'

He gave me his name and address and hung up.

I felt angry at having given in to the blackmail, especially since I had hoped to stay behind for a while with Martha after surgery hours. But in the event it was she who induced me, without knowing it, to keep my appointment with the sick man.

'I'm sorry, Doctor, but I won't be able to come in tomorrow,' she whispered as the last patient was leaving. 'I'm getting married at half past ten, and in the afternoon . . . '

As I heard this I was tempted to take her in my arms and exercise my dominance over her, to claim my rightful *droit de seigneur*. Fortunately I was able to control myself.

I was surprised to hear myself saying: 'Right, I have to hurry. I've an urgent case to visit. I just might be able to save his life. Congratulations, and see you the day after tomorrow. Don't forget to turn off all the lights.'

Half an hour later I was back in the old district where I grew up. The houses, once luxurious, now seemed lifeless ruins, but quite without any sense of tragedy. Crumbling plaster, patched up window panes, rotten wooden beams propping up courtyards and entrance halls. Tiny human beings wrapped up from head to foot scurried about on broken pavements. Every now and again they would stop for a little rest, moving on after five or six breaths.

Twenty years had gone by since I had last set foot in the Eighth District, still in the central part of town. I crossed Karfenstein Street, skirted past the market on Teleky Square and turned into People's Theatre Street. I entered the apartment block as directed by my troublesome patient-to-be.

Inside, I came face to face with the statue of a boy, of decidedly mediocre manufacture, and his eyes followed my progress across the hallway to a rickety elevator. On the fourth floor I had to walk all the way around the internal balcony, its wooden handrail supported on wrought iron railings painted an oily black.

Number five was an apartment whose windows faced in towards the courtyard. The glass door faced in the same direction.

I pushed the plastic bell button and the door was opened by a little old lady with thinning white hair, wearing a grease-stained dress with a faded pattern of red flowers. At that instant I recalled my new patient's mention of his two brothers. And as I entered the

143

darkened apartment I came face to face with all three in an old family photograph hanging framed in the hallway.

I saw three boys sitting in a row with their arms folded, each wearing the radiant expression that I have never been able to define properly. The woman who had just shown me in I recognized immediately as their mother; she was sitting somewhat to the right of the three in the photograph, a little cut off from them and was the only one looking at the camera, wearing a sad and strangely allusive expression, almost as if she was sharing a secret with the viewer.

'Thank you, Doctor, thank you,' the old woman began, handing me a bundle of rags made up to look like a fancy parcel. 'Please don't be offended, it was my poor husband's. I thought you might like it.' I opened the bundle and took out a pocket watch, apparently made of solid gold. 'Please accept it, Doctor. You've been so good to my sons—may the earth not find them a burden—you looked after them so well, the poor things. Now it's the turn of the third. I don't have anyone else. Come, come and examine him.'

I showed an appropriate degree of reticence before accepting the present, but finally I concluded that it was merely a surrogate, no different from the fee which you pay today for practically everything, even a simple doctor's prescription. The poor woman obviously had no money and she must have thought long and hard before sacrificing the watch.

We entered the darkened bedroom the sole window of which opened on to the courtyard.

'Good day, Doctor. Excuse me if I don't get up, but you can see my condition. You did so much for my brothers, now I hope you'll help me. Do you remember them? One came to you ten years ago, the other fifteen or twenty, I don't remember any more. It was just after the war. Or maybe it was just after the revolution. I don't know.'

And then in the darkness of that little room, for the third time in so many years, I had the sensation of confronting someone surrounded by an aura of luminosity. Every aspect of him, every visible part of his body, was suffused with an air of solemn joyfulness, as if in expectation of some great event, the very proximity of which caused an irresistible euphoria.

The mother stood at the foot of the bed, watching over the invalid with a look of admiration and great tenderness. But the instant she turned away from him and looked towards me, her expression changed. A blank look of resigned objectivity spread across her face, in which, even at that age (she must have been about eighty), one could still detect the sweet and melancholy beauty of long ago. The photograph in the hall showed her with shining dark hair, white teeth and a penetrating look with just the hint of a sparkle in her pupils.

Now she was standing in front of me, leaning on a metal cane, pale, her narrow shoulders sagging. She smiled at me.

'You look after him, Doctor, the way you looked after the other two. You're such a good man.'

Good? What had I done to save those two men, or even to help them? And where was the second? Whatever had become of him? But the old woman spared me the awkward question by continuing: 'The second . . . you understand . . . Fifteen years ago. Ah, yes, how time flies by . . . '

'He died of a heart attack,' the remaining brother explained, 'but he had arterial stenosis in his legs. In the end he was unable to move from one side of the room to the other. I even had to carry him to the toilet. And now it's my turn. Look, look at this swelling here, in my right leg. It is so painful. Let me die quickly Doctor. You are so good.'

So the family had chosen me as their judge, but I could pass only one sentence: the penalty of death. The judgement had been handed down before either they or I had been born, and there was no appeal. The solemnity, the luminous aura was that of the sacrificial victim. And by agreeing to the visit I had accepted the role, however much it conflicted with my personal and professional ethics. It was too late now to turn back. There was only one thing I could do.

I had the patient undress and I began my examination. The swelling in the right leg near the ankle could have been a symptom of any number of organic disorders. However I was able to exclude diabetes, malignancy, and malfunctions of the kidneys and of the circulatory system from the list of possible causes.

'Sciatica, rheumatism or a simple injury,' I pronounced in tones of triumphal certainty. 'Don't worry, you certainly won't die of this illness.' Naturally I was happy to be able to give a hopeful diagnosis every now and then.

'Did you say I'll get better?' the invalid said, with an almost imperceptible hint of disappointment in his voice.

'Yes. The cure will not be easy, but you will get better, I can assure you of that.'

'But can it be cured, Doctor?'

'Yes. Some illnesses are transitory, and yours is one of those.'

'Are you being serious? There really are such things as transitory illnesses?'

'Yes.' I put an end to the discussion, suspecting I wasn't going to be able to convince them of the truth of what I was saying. 'And now I have to go.' In that instant I heard a feeble noise behind me, like the sound of someone sighing. I turned around. The mother was standing behind my back, sobbing tearlessly, but all the more desperately for that. Her shoulders, so narrow in relation to her hips, were shaking under a storm of inexpressible emotions.

'You astonish me,' she gasped, each syllable an effort to catch her breath in the turmoil of the moment. 'You astonish me. You're not content with having killed two of my children, now, heaven forbid, you want to take my last from me? Have you not even a spark of conscience? Can you not see what a state that leg is in? Even a newborn child would realize that my son's life is in danger. Either help him or let him die in peace, Doctor. I never thought I'd say this to you Doctor, but after all . . . How dare you claim that my son isn't seriously ill?'

Then it all became clear to me. The woman expected me to take responsibility for the death of the third son in addition to the other two. No remission was possible. If it came to it I would have to kill him. Yes, that was it: she wanted me to kill him. Not judge, but executioner, that was the part she wanted me to play.

The swelling was in all three cases the symptom of a completely different illness, but one that had struck each man in the same limb: the right leg. In view of the enormous progress medical science has made over the last few decades I know that it is madness to lose oneself in philosophical speculation of this sort, but Professor Bahdy's paper made me realize that forms of illness and even causes of death are no more than symbols. It is not the mechanism itself which is important (except insofar as we are able to intervene to change its course) but rather that which the mechanism is trying to express. Seen like this, our lives might only be the relatively insignificant preamble to the unique truth towards which we are all heading, the only indications of which are the illnesses of our bodies and, definitively, our own deaths

Behind the radiant respectability of the three brothers I detected an inexplicable silence. Their own lives remained incomprehensible even to them. Their only possibility of communication was through the expression of their sickness and the form of their deaths.

The little old woman would not let go and continued to sob disconsolately.

Can I risk a hypothesis? These three brothers sacrificed themselves for a love which demanded such a sacrifice. What this love might have hidden, and what kind of love it was, are questions too difficult to comprehend, much less answer.

After this visit, which I ended in indignation, my career took a downward turn. Old enmities and petty jealousies deprived me of my chair at the university. But I bear no grudges now. A doctor, after all, seeks the truth. Philosophers gave that up some time ago. The current state of science gives me grounds for hope, but only hope. Without the certainty of truth, I am unable to practice science. That is why I am giving it up. I will keep the gold watch, and wait.

E.D.P

Professor Bahdy, 'A Lower Limb Disease', *Asiatic Medical Researches*, number 4, 1985

Professor E. D. Puster, 'Statistics about Bahdy's Disease and Chromosome Y Mutation', New York, 1988

CHOICES

St John's hospital covers a vast area, right in the heart of the First District, but its wards, which seem to be in a state of perpetual transformation, are connected by narrow, dusty corridors.

Eugene Shermann was brought here in a very serious condition. The original diagnosis, still in the archives, speaks of sarcomatosis.

He was moved into a room with six beds, in each of which lay a silent, well disciplined patient. Every day his wife Erna brought him his lunch from home. They would talk, exchange trivialities, gossip about the other residents in their apartment block on Wednesday Street. Then Erna would gather together the plates and the bowls, wave goodbye to Eugene and disappear swiftly down the passageway. She was sixty-five, he was seventy-two. They had been together for more than forty years.

They had got to know each other at a local dance, just after the end of what the history books now call the First

World War. He was already completely bald, with a substantial paunch. She was small and plump, with thick black hair gathered in around her neck. Her large eyes would open and close as if she was giving way to an overwhelming sleepiness whenever the person she was with began to bore her or otherwise failed to meet expectations. By the time she met Eugene she had already devastated one suitor, Ladislav Schwarz, a book-keeper at a firm of importers of tropical fruit. For a whole year Ladislav had gone to meet her every afternoon outside the women's fashions boutique in Vac Street where she worked as a seamstress, then walked her home to Karfenstein Street. They walked arm-in-arm, chatting about any old thing to avoid having nothing to say to each other. But after a time, Erna decided he was too beautiful for her. For as they walked home, Ladislav would keep turning around and staring at other girls, and the other girls stared back at him.

'Please don't come for me ever again,' Erna told him one day, without further explanation. 'I'm perfectly capable of going home by myself.' So Ladislav Schwarz disappeared from her life. And Erna wrote down the date in her diary: 20 March 1920.

The typographer Eugene Shermann was a rather awkward and overly formal sort of man. He lived with his mother whom he had been supporting since he was twelve years old. He was taken on as an apprentice at the typesetters and a few years later was promoted to machine compositor.

He was a swift worker; no one else could set as many ens per hour as he could. Typographical errors were unknown to him. He could decipher the most garbled manuscripts. And no spelling mistake ever escaped him, no matter how deeply buried in the work of some poet or novelist. He would sit at his machine for thirteen, fourteen hours a day. With his pliers he would pull the tiny pieces of lead, each one embossed with a letter, from the packed wooden cases, and from there slide them into position in lines of type. The thoughts enclosed in each symbol by his own two hands danced before his eyes; and messages born in dark rooms would find their way in the hands of other people into sumptuous buildings. Eugene sipped every now and again from a glass of milk placed on a chair. The milk was supposed to guard against lead poisoning. The monotonous clicking of the composing machine rang in his ears at night, providing a background to the sound of his sick mother's sighing and moaning. One day Shermann the typographer wrote a poem on this concerto of noises, full of melancholy and resignation.

As a boy he had supplemented his earnings performing every Thursday afternoon on the outer circle of People's Park as assistant to a fourth-rate magician. He would rehearse their tricks, changed every two or three months, on Saturday and Sunday mornings, getting up even earlier than usual. He learned to throw his voice and to imitate the sounds of a trumpet and a balalaika.

By the time he reached thirty the entire neighbourhood had taken to calling him simply 'Baldy' and he took pleasure in his nickname, rubbing his billiard ball-smooth head every time he heard his name mentioned.

His third source of income, and also occasionally of loss, was horse-racing. Every Friday and Saturday afternoon, armed with binoculars and specialist newspapers, he would go to the old race-track to place his bet. If he came home with money it was celebrations all round: sweets for his little nephews and his sisters and for the whole family a ride around town in a horse-drawn carriage or an afternoon at the Café Emke drinking hot chocolate and eating cake. When he lost he would come home and go to bed without a word.

But apart from the horses, Eugene Shermann's only vice was his habit of eating unthinkable quantities of whatever he could get into his stomach. It is hard to say whether his voracity was of a pathological nature. There was no mention of it in his medical records, nor in the yellowing prescriptions found lying in a wicker basket at his home. Nevertheless it was more than just a simple fact of his character; more probably some kind of irresistible imperative, something he was born with, stronger than his own will, stronger even than the laws of life itself. This overpowering impulse drove him to feed himself continuously, at any and every hour of the day, with the result that his stomach was permanently full of food and gas. To find temporary relief from the torment of indigestion he would often call in the children of his neighbours or of his sister and get them to do a little dance on his bare back, 'to straighten out the bones,' as he used to say, but more probably to help him release the wind from his belly. This happened often, much to the amusement of the children.

And it was like this, through an open door, that Erna, his wife-to-be, saw him for the first time. She had come to deliver a newly made suit to Eugene's neighbour.

At that time the Shermann family lived on Wednesday Street, in an apartment block full of Gypsies. Erna lived on Karfenstein Street. The prostitutes of Conti Street, for whom she, so chaste and demure, had learned to make working clothes which were, to say the least, on the provocative side expected her to come by every morning. And so she passed along Wednesday Street every day. Eugene Shermann would stare after her from the single window in his tiny, dark apartment at the end of the alley.

In those days they had all kinds of ceremonies which are unknown today: balls, engagement parties, official marriage requests. Both Eugene and Erna went along to a ball organized by the Jews of the Eighth District, each intending to come away engaged. Erna couldn't dance, and spent the entire evening in the darkest corner of the hall keeping her sisters company. Whoever wanted to find her knew where to look. Erna put her trust in destiny, that is, in the will of the Almighty.

Eugene Shermann found her. She said yes immediately. His lack of physical attractiveness was Erna's guarantee that their marriage would remain free of the cloying emotions of lovers and sweethearts. Her older brothers—Erna was an orphan—gave her permission to get married, and she gave up her job at the women's fashions boutique and started to work regularly making dresses for the prostitutes. She sewed on her old Singer under the window from which Eugene used to spy on her. She looked after his old mother who was ill with a bone tumour, helped her to die and the day after the funeral took her place in bed. Until then she had slept on the floor, between Eugene's bed and her mother-in-law's.

From her only union with Eugene, which took place at the end of the week of mourning, she gave birth to a son who was brought up in an atmosphere of love and severity.

Eugene was not a believer; he had even got involved in the socialist trade union at the typographers. Erna in her own way was religious and observant.

'My son,' Eugene said to the boy on the day of his bar mitzvah, 'I've had this ring specially made for you. The decoration, see, on both sides, I designed. The stone too, an emerald—I chose it.'

'And I saved the money to buy it,' said Erna, 'sewing

night and day. Just so you know that into this ring went all my effort, all my hours, all my thoughts. Take great care of it, and may God be a help to you.'

The boy, whose official name was Frederic, but who was called Aaron by the community, looked at the ring for a long time before trying it on at the door of the temple.

'It's too big!' he exclaimed anxiously.

'It will fit you perfectly once you've grown big enough,' said his father. 'Try it on once a month and you'll see.' And for the first time in his life he leaned down and kissed the boy.

Those three beings, their lives joined in the belly of that dark building, were visited one day by the poisonous currents of war and persecution. They were taken away, separated, then reunited again. The moment of their destruction, all at once or one at a time, never arrived. They survived the war.

Erna offered up prayer after prayer of thanksgiving; Eugene put it all down to the nemesis of history: many innocents, but also many evildoers, had been spared in that whirlpool of blood.

Aaron wore the ring on the day he first turned up for work, he too at the typographers. He began to go around with the girls of the district. He was now old enough to start thinking of having a family of his own. The day he packed his clothes and the few possessions he needed to go off and live an independent life, Eugene was terribly agitated. He devoured everything he could lay his hands on in the kitchen, while Erna turned the wheel on her old machine, sewing more joyfully than usual.

'Even the birds, once their wings are fledged, fly away from the nest,' she said. 'The Lord ordained it that way. So don't be silly. Come to bed now.' They lay in each other's arms that night, and Eugene's heavy breath reminded Erna of the sweet milky smell of her son when he was little.

'Erna, come quickly,' Eugene said, pulling his wife along with him to the toilet, which was in a corner of the courtyard next to the back staircase. 'I don't know what's happening to me. Look.'

It was a few days after Frederic had said goodbye. The toilet bowl was covered in blood. A pile of faeces lay at the bottom like the decomposing corpse of a new-born baby.

With his wife's help, Eugene's haemorrhoids (that's what he thought they were) got better, and for a while he was well. He retired from his job at the typographers. Then a few weeks after his last day at work he was admitted to St John's Hospital for an operation on his rectum. He was fitted with a bag to wear at his side in which the waste products of his digestion would accumulate. Eugene had to try to keep this bag clean.

His son visited him often, but Eugene detected in him a sense of fear, or worse, revulsion, which made him cry at night in the dimly lit hospital ward. Erna left her dressmaking at three o'clock every day and walked from Wednesday Street to the hospital, praying for him all the way. She prayed calmly, without desperation.

Her husband was discharged, and not long after arriving home began to apply himself to the household chores. He would cook and clean, while Erna got on with her dressmaking, no longer for the inhabitants of the brothels—these had been abolished by the new government—but for other women whose requirements were less pointed, but all the more secure for that. Erna devoted much attention and imagination to bringing out every aspect of femininity in her clients, just as she denied it in herself. She went to them in the spirit of one who visits the sick, to do a good deed.

Then the country revolted, and this was followed by a counter-revolution. The people who organized the counter-revolution accused the original revolutionaries of being counter-revolutionaries and, having won, proclaimed themselves the real revolutionaries.

Eugene puzzled over these happenings with Erna for hours on end. He was a knowledgeable man, but finally, after endless discussion, he could only ascribe such violent changes to the unstoppable onward course of history. He would picture the onward course of history to himself as an immense river, down which floated so many boats full of human beings. Erna imagined the will of the Almighty as a giant fist thumping an enormous table.

In those tumultuous days Aaron came to visit them. He was in a rather solemn and mysterious mood.

'This place is not for me. You know what I mean, don't you, Dad? I want to be rich, and here you're not allowed to be rich. You know how quick-tempered I am, how I don't weigh my words very carefully. Here if you say certain things they stick you in gaol. So I've decided to leave, just as soon as I'm able. It'll have to be soon, before all this hullabaloo has quietened down. I know nothing of revolution and counter-revolution. All I know is that I want to be rich.'

Eugene and Erna remained silent for a long time. This was not how a good son should speak to his parents, and that counted for more than anything else in their family.

'I've brought the ring,' Aaron continued after a painful silence, 'not because I want to give it back, but for you to have as a reminder of me and as a token of my intention to come back one day and take you with me, so that we'll all be back together again as one family in another part of the world.'

'We'll never see each other again,' said Eugene, who had asked a lot of questions of the doctors and knew well what fate awaited him. And then he added: 'You're a grown man, you know what you're doing. May the Lord bless your footsteps.' He took back the ring he had given his son, kissed his forehead and didn't address another word to him for the rest of the evening.

Aaron left at dawn the next day and Eugene watched him go from the window of the tiny apartment on Wednesday Street. Outside on Matyas Square they had dug communal graves for dead of the revolution and the counter-revolution. Aaron had to pass by the graves to get to the lorry which was waiting at the corner of the square to take him far away from his native land.

From that day on Eugene was never the same again. Although he loved and respected his wife and treated her with a rather clumsy formality, he would now lose his temper from time to time, and answer rudely back at her. When this happened little Erna would stop, wipe her hands in her apron, fix him with her eyes, and say: 'Are you crazy, Eugene?' Then she would lower her eyelids, shutting him out of her world.

Eugene Shermann began, more assiduously than before, to frequent the races, but now he no longer stopped at betting small sums. It was as if he wanted to bring about his own downfall before the Almighty ordered him to leave the chessboard. Eugene would sometimes lay half of his pension on one bet, until one day he bet the whole of it and lost.

Leaving the race-track he didn't know where to go. He didn't have the courage to tell Erna how he had brought disgrace down upon his head. He wandered about the city, his great paunch thrusting out before him, his bald head bobbing up and down in the grey crowds. He began humming to himself in desperation. Suddenly he had an idea. He smacked his forehead and set off quickly back home. After greeting Erna with his usual affectionate respect he went straight off to bed. Erna, who was waiting with his supper, looked long and hard at him, then decided not to ask any questions that day.

The next morning Eugene was up and out by seven. Erna woke and looked all around for him. 'Where has that *meschügge* got to now?' she muttered, dressing hastily. 'He wouldn't be playing some trick on me, would he? You can't get any peace and quiet in this life.'

She searched for him in the market, in the cafés, in the shops, she even telephoned his old workplace, the typographers. She took the thirty-six tram to the corner of People's Theatre Street. Then, just as she was about to get on the number six to the East Station, she stopped. She knotted her headscarf under her chin and said to herself: 'I'm not going to let him drive me crazy, that's for sure. Why all the fuss? If he wants to act like a madman, why should I follow suit?'

She turned around and began to walk home. As she passed by the grey building on the corner of Adam Vaj Street, the sound of a guitar reached her ears. Drawn by her own curiosity rather than by the unusual sound, Erna went into the courtyard. There in the middle, standing on yellow tiles, his hat by his feet, his bald head held up high against the black railings, Eugene Shermann was imitating the sounds of a guitar and a mandolin. An audience of toothless pensioners and astonished children watched the busker's impromptu performance from various floors in the building. Two or three coins fell, bouncing and rolling nearby.

'Have you gone mad?' Erna shouted, seizing her husband by the jacket. 'Come away this minute! For shame! The things I have to put up with in my life!'

'Erna, dearest,' Eugene replied, following his wife like a puppy, 'I obviously owe you an explanation, and you'll get it in time.'

'There's nothing to explain,' said Erna with a note of finality, as she continued to drag her husband, whose eyes were by now popping and brimful of tears with the pain, along the street towards home. 'The only thing to do is to go away and hide, and *schluss*!'

'You're right, I'm thoroughly ashamed of myself,' whispered Eugene as he crossed the threshold of the house in Wednesday Street. 'I've lost all my dignity—and all my money. I bet it away on the horses.'

Erna stopped, gave a deep sigh and said: 'May it all turn out for the best.' She stood still for a moment, then started off again, but not as quickly now.

Later that day Eugene felt a tremendous pain in his back as he lay down so that he had to spend the night lying on his front, with his stomach in continual agitation under the weight. After a week the pain had become unbearable and they had to call a doctor.

'You should prepare yourself for the worst,' the doctor told Erna after the examination. 'It has metastasized to the bone, I'm sure. There's a small chance I could be wrong.'

'Metastasized? What does that mean?' Erna asked.

'Madam, the disease your husband had before in his rectum has now moved to his bones. I wouldn't wish it on my worst enemy.'

'Why did He invent all these tortures?'

'Who?'

'I know who,' she replied, raising her eyes to the heavens. Then she lowered her eyelids, as if with this rather emphatic gesture she could abolish heaven itself.

Eugene was taken off to hospital, and at the same time the first letters began to arrive from Aaron in far-off Canada.

'Everything's beautiful here, everything's new,' he wrote. 'The only thing missing is you.' Erna read the letter to her husband, now frighteningly thin and weak, writhing in his hospital bed.

'I have to go home,' Eugene murmured when he heard those words.

'Go home? Have you gone mad? What would you do at home, with you in so much pain?'

'I want to say goodbye to him, for the last time.'

'Who do you want to say goodbye to?'

'Aaron.'

'Now come on! Aren't you too old for such nonsense? You know very well that Aaron is in Ottawa, on the other side of the ocean. Do you want to fly over to see him?'

'No, I don't have the money for the journey.'

'Exactly. So what do you want to go home for?'

'To say goodbye. To the ring.'

Erna was struck dumb. She fixed him with her big grey eyes. 'I'll bring it to you,' she said solemnly.

'No, please, not here, not into the midst of all this sickness. It might get infected.'

Eugene fell back on the bed, exhausted by the effort of talking so much, of wanting so much. Erna stayed by him until he dozed off, then she tucked in his sheets and left the ward, taking her leave politely of the other patients. They responded with weak, tearful goodbyes.

When she returned the following afternoon, Erna found Eugene sitting up on the side of the bed wearing all his clothes.

'They've allowed me to leave. Let's go.'

'Will you manage on foot?'

'Of course I'll manage, angel,' Eugene whispered, and he set off with shaky steps. Erna took him by the arm without a word.

Once home she made him sit down on a stool in the kitchen. The tiny apartment hummed with the faint noises of the afternoon.

'Would you like a coffee?'

'No, thank you, angel,' Eugene answered, and turned his head towards the room. Erna understood the significance of this slight movement. She went to the cupboard and opened one of the doors. She reached in with her arm, ignoring the shelves bursting with sheets, pillowcases and towels, all folded neatly and drowned in a strong odour of naphthalene. She groped to one side and then the other, then from under a pile of never-worn nightshirts, she pulled a red leather-covered box.

'There you are, since you care so much about it. I only hope the Lord doesn't let any evil come of it.'

Erna opened the lid of the box. The ring, with its great green stone, flashed in the darkness of the kitchen. Eugene put it in the palm of his hand, and Erna put the coffee on. Eugene's bulging eyes filled with tears. 'Be good to your mother, since you weren't good to me,' murmured the typographer. He put the ring back in the box and closed the lid.

The X-ray plates developed over the following two weeks showed a diminution of the opaque area which corresponded to the spread of the tumour. During that fortnight Eugene had peaceful and triumphant dreams, and he and Erna talked together about the future and about the possibility of going to visit their son. It was the happiest time of their lives. The doctors were astounded, speechless. Then one day Eugene had an attack of excruciating pains in his spine.

A week after this he entered the terminal phase of his illness. Shooting pains ran through all his bones, as if the framework of his clumsy construction of flesh was threatening to collapse and leave a formless mass, deprived of support and of dignity.

Eugene implored the doctors to give him an injection which would put an end to it all instantly. 'I'm sorry, but our professional ethics do not permit it,' was Dr Klein's firm response, taking the dying man's hand in his.

Then one day Erna arrived with a letter from their son. She had written to him about his father's condition, and warned him of his imminent death. Aaron didn't know how to address his father: in the face of such a solemn event, one of greater significance than any other instant in one's own or anyone else's life, all he could find to write was: 'Here the weather is fine; the sun is shining and it's not at all windy.'

'Yes, yes, the sun is shining over there, but for me it is evening,' Eugene said, his eyes full of tears. 'Look, Erna dear, from here down'—and he pointed to his side with a tired wave of his hand—'I'm already dead. Only here am I still alive,' and he indicated his chest, 'and here in my head. But not for much longer.' After an hour of silence he added, 'I'm grateful to you for everything,' then fell asleep.

'What are you doing here?' demanded the duty doctor of Erna who was staring fixedly at her husband's face.

'Visiting hours finished some time ago. Why don't you go home. Tomorrow morning you'll get a telegram. Your husband won't survive the night.'

Erna took the letter, tucked it into Eugene's pyjamas, gave a hundred florin note to the doctor and then turned to the invalid who was by now in a coma. 'Well, goodbye then.'

Eugene seemed shrunken, as if an irresistible force had pulled all the molecules of his body in towards a single point where all his pain was concentrated. Erna lowered her eyelids and left.

At Eugene's funeral she said a prayer on behalf of their son, then she approached the coffin and murmured in a quiet voice: 'Take me away from here. Do you hear me? Goodbye for now.' She didn't shed a single tear. 'I can't cry,' she said, as if to excuse herself to the rabbi who, so everyone said, was in the habit of eating a couple of onions or one or two cloves of garlic before making a funeral oration.

Not many months after this Aaron wrote her a letter full of bitterness, confessing all his failures, his inability to get on in life without the help of those who taught him everything he knew. 'Come over here to this wonderful country, we'll live together and you'll have everything you want, even if I never become rich.'

Erna loved her son and she cried long and hard when she read the letter. She went to the cemetery and sat down next to her husband's still fresh grave and began to reason with him.

'A little while ago I asked you to take me with you. Life without you and without Aaron seemed meaningless to me then. You'll have to forgive me, but I've come to ask you for an extension. I've changed my mind—I want to stay here. Maybe not for long, just to come here and chat to you, perhaps make a dress for a some girl or other—I'm still good with my hands. The fact of the matter is I want to see things, feel things from down here, not from up there. I don't need a lot: a coffee with milk, a little bread and butter, a biscuit or two, does me for a whole day. Somebody might need me, one of my sisters perhaps; you know how I like helping the sick, how it doesn't upset me at all. And who knows, even you might need me, from up there. I'll never forget you. There, and now I'll have to get home. There's a bit of tidying to do and I have to write a nice letter to Aaron. By the way, he wants me to go and live with him. What do you say to that?'

And in this way Erna finally worked up the courage to broach the subject with him. Then she stood for a long time in silence, listening, and going over her own thoughts. At dusk she walked back along the dusty road from that remote spot in the Stone Quarry district and took the tram back into town. She spent the entire journey working out word for word in her head the text of the letter she would send to Canada. Once home she

171

took paper and pencil, put on her spectacles, sat down and began to write.

Dear Aaron,
You asked me to make a choice. I've been to talk with your father and I've asked him for an extension. I have always admired your father: he was an honest man, hard-working, he never showed me anything but respect, and he always gave me all his pay. Honesty and respect mean everything to me, they are the real proof of love. You too are an honest boy, if a bit headstrong. May the Almighty help you. My place is here: that is my choice. Your father needs me. I'll think of you always, but I'll never leave here, I'll always stay close to your father, to the piece of earth where he rests. But let us change the subject. The weather is fine here and the sun is shining. What's it like with you? Write to me soon. Goodbye, and may the Almighty bless your footsteps.

Erna is ninety-eight years old. Her love for her husband and her son are 'a memorial' according to Dr Klein, who has been treating her for thirty years for mildly oscillating blood pressure.

'Sarcoma Generale Regressum', in *Review of Oncology*, Siracuse (Canada) and Jerusalem, 1958
Interviews on Regressed Cancer Cases, New York, 1987